WICKED POTION

THE ROYAL: WITCH COURT BOOK 4

MEGAN MONTERO

LEO PRESS

For Aunt Nancy,
Thank you for introducing me to the world I love so much,
without you my imagination never would've taken flight.
Xoxo-Megan

The Royals: Witch Court Season 1

Wicked Witch

Wicked Magic

Wicked Hex

Wicked Potion

Wicked Queen

The Royals: Warlock Court Season 2

Wicked Omen- Coming 2018

Beckett's face crumpled as he gazed down at his watch. His brows drew low over his ocean-blue eyes, and he pressed his lips into a thin line. When he dropped his arms to his sides, he looked away from me. I narrowed my eyes at him over my shoulder. She had to wake up. There was no other choice. "Beckett, time?"

He shook his head and ran his hand through his surfer blond hair. Tremors rocked me as I shot to my feet and turned to face him. She had to be okay. She was my everything. "How much longer?"

His breath hitched in his throat. "Time's up." He gazed past me toward Zinnia.

I launched myself forward and wrapped my hands in his shirt, then shoved him up against the wall. My breath caught in my throat, and a sharp pain shot through my chest. *I need her to be okay. She has to be okay.* "Check it again!"

"Tuck, time was up five minutes ago."

When his gaze met mine, I knew he was telling the truth, but I didn't want to hear it. I refused to believe him. *She is not gone.* "I said look again!"

He shook his head.

"Do it, damn it!"

I haven't even gotten the chance to tell her how I really felt, and now she may never know.

All the time I'd wasted hiding what we were to each other, for what? It was never meant to be this way. We were only teenagers. We had the rest of our lives to be together . . . *I thought.*

I turned back toward her lifeless body. Her once shining porcelain skin now held a blueish tinge. I stared at her chest, willing it to move, praying she would suck in just one breath and wake from the potion she'd taken to save me. I reached out and brushed my fingers through her wild midnight hair. I bent down low and whispered in her ear, "Come on, babe. You can't leave me now, not so soon."

Still, she didn't move. Dizziness overcame me, and I felt my heart being ripped from my chest. A single tear rolled down the side of my face as I buried it in her neck. "Please wake up, for me. For us."

My arms shook as I wrapped them around Zinnia's limp body. I pulled her into my chest, clutching her closer to me. I rocked her back and forth, hoping just to see a small spark of life.

This is my fault.

If I hadn't fallen under Alataris' hex, none of this would've happened. Zinnia would still be alive, Ophelia wouldn't be behind these walls, and we would be further in the fight against Alataris.

It should be me . . . not her. Oh God, I wish it were me.

I couldn't picture a world without her. I inhaled her warm vanilla scent, making sure to burn it into my memory. The muscles in my body all tightened at the same time, and I shook with the effort it took not to squeeze her too hard.

I had nothing else to lose in this world. All that mattered was Zinnia, and she was gone. I rose to my feet and lifted her up off the cot, with one arm under her knees and the other supporting her torso. Her body was limp, her arms hung out to her sides, and her head lolled back. Those midnight locks I loved to run my fingers through swayed and brushed my knees. I was desperate to see her sapphire eyes. I wanted to watch them spark with life or narrow at me in frustration.

I let everything inside of me go. The aching burn, the unending hurt, pain, regret, I released it all. Flames shot from my skin, and I prayed for once that they would consume me. My family? She was my family. This world? Nothing without her. My friends? How could I look at them now knowing I'd taken her away from them? She was my soul mate, my everything. Where she went, I would follow. One way or another, I would find her again. The pain was too much. My flaming wings erupted from my back, and I spread them out wide. I threw my head back, and for the first time in my life, I let my inner blaze go. The rage I felt toward my parents casting me out, the pain of hurting my soul mate, the frustration of being trapped in a world where she didn't exist . . . I let it all go and just . . . burned.

White hot flames flared down my back, across my chest, and onto my arms. My body turned into one continuous scorching bonfire, and I let it. I wanted to turn to ash with her, to be with her in the end. Pain like I'd never felt ripped through my chest, the pain of losing her too soon. We'd barely just begun.

I turned around to face Beckett. He held his hand up, blocking his eyes from the volcanic flames shooting out from my body. The rocky floor beneath me turned molten, and my feet sank down. I didn't stop. I needed to let everything I felt scorch out of me until I could feel nothing at all. If my flames hadn't vaporized each of my tears away, they would stain my face.

As I held her in my arms, I knew her body couldn't take much more of this, but I'd be damned if I saw her lying in a coffin buried where she couldn't feel the warmth of the sun or the cool of snow. No, my Zinnia would be freed and spread among the world she loved so much. The world that would be dimmer without her in it. I dropped to my knees, feeling as though I was nearly out of power. The fire I let loose was burning off any of the energy I had left in me. I was being sucked dry.

It can't be.

That's when I felt it deep in my chest—something I didn't think I'd ever feel again . . . a siphoning.

CHAPTER 2

Time's up? He can't be serious! There's no way it all ends like this. No way I'd lose my best friend like this.

I stood motionless, watching as Tucker's body ignited into a blazing inferno. I sucked in deep, panting breaths. I saw this the second my hand brushed hers— her downfall, his pain.

Why didn't I try harder to warn her?

I stumbled back a step, and Grayson caught me by the arm. The others should be here, not recuperating in the infirmary from getting attacked by Tuck the night before. They needed to be here to witness what Ophelia had done to us all.

Grayson glanced around the room. "That's not it. Bloody hell, this can't be it." He swiped his hand over his face. His chocolate eyes were locked on Zinnia as he backed up against the wall. "I don't know about you lot, but no." He shook his head. "There's no way she's not waking up."

Even I could hear the doubt in his voice. The breath stuck between my lips, and my chest was caving in on me.

I can't breathe. I can't breathe.

I shoved out of Grayson's grip and wiped at my face. Hot tears flowed down my cheeks. Each one seared my face, scorching this moment into my memory. The only close friend I had in this world lay lifeless in Tucker's arms. He cradled her and rocked her back and forth, all the while burning brighter. The life that used to shine within her was gone. Her head lolled back, and strands of her wild midnight hair drifted over his arm. Tiny flames danced through the strands yet never burned her.

Tucker's dark auburn locks fell forward, covering his features. After he'd barely survived the hex plaguing him, he looked like he'd just fought a battle. His shirt was ripped and torn, exposing patches of his tan skin. The phoenix tattoo on his neck glowed a soft ember. Did it change with his mood? I didn't know, but now even I could feel the sadness rolling off of him.

His face was buried in her neck, but I could still hear his quiet sobs. His words were soft, pleading, and insistent. "Don't die, please God. Don't die."

My knees buckled and slammed into the ground. I didn't want her to die! The sound of my own crying flooded my ears. Desperate gasps scratched my throat, and I tried to catch my breath. I hunched over and spread my fingers out on the cold stone floor. We were still in the jail cell where only moments ago Tuck was going insane because of a wicked hex. Now he would live because of her, because of the sacrifice she'd just made. The ultimate sacrifice. Zinnia Heart, our Queen Siphon Witch, had killed herself to save him. The guy she obsessed over.

No, she didn't kill herself . . . Ophelia killed her.

Zinnia put her trust in O, and now she was gone from this world.

My magic gathered in my fingertips. I snapped my head up and met Ophelia's wide-eyed gaze. "You *killed* her." The words were a growl through my gritted teeth.

I knew what I looked like—face covered in red blotches, thick black makeup streaming down my tear-stained cheeks, and sparks of my purple magic running over my arms.

Ophelia took a step back. Her obsidian eyes swam with tears. "It wasn't supposed to be like this. The potion—"

"Didn't work! *Murderer.*" The ground rumbled beneath my feet, and I felt the dead move to my command. I was Queen of the Dead, and it was about time I embraced it! They listened to me. I'd once feared my power; now I let it loose. Strands of my white blond hair blew back from my face. "I don't think it was an accident! You were planted here by your father, and now you did exactly what you meant to do."

Large tears rolled down her face as she waved her hands in front of her, trying to ward me off. "Nova, we're friends. You have to believe me. I love Zinnia. I would never do anything to hurt her."

I shook my head. "Lies! It's all lies!"

The ground exploded, sending dirt flying in all directions. Reanimates surged from the cracks in the cell floor. Their zombie-like features were contorted in soundless screams as they reached out toward Ophelia with skeletal hands. A sneer tugged at my lips as I forced them to rise from the underworld to come and claim her. Ophelia turned from me and tried to run down the hall, but my Reanimates blocked her from escaping. They swarmed in behind her, covering the doorway leading out.

I pressed my lips into a hard line and fought the sob about to escape my throat. "What did you think would happen? You'd come in and kill one of us and walk away?"

Ophelia spun in a circle. Her curtain of black hair fell

from the messy bun on her head and fanned out around her shoulders. I could almost smell the terror pouring off of her. She took another step back, trying to push through to the other side of the doorway. "I'm telling you. I didn't kill her."

It was too late. I had her surrounded. More Reanimates clawed their way from the crack in the ground. There were at least a dozen of them now. Usually, I would be gagging just from the sight of their decomposing flesh, the smell of their rotting skin, and their thirst for violence. But Ophelia had taken my closest friend, and she had to pay. I held my hand up, commanding them to grab her. Purple sparks lit up the jail cell like fireworks on the Fourth of July.

I heard Beckett screaming something, but I was too focused on taking out Ophelia, the girl who stole my bestie from me, the one friend who got me. With one potion, Ophelia killed any chance we had of defeating Alataris for good. The Reanimates grabbed at her arms and legs. Ophelia threw her arms up and twisted out of their grip, breaking free.

"Not so fast." I shot to my feet and lifted my arms over my head.

Skeleton arms sprouted from the ground like weeds. Their boney fingers wrapped around her ankles and legs, holding her in place. Ophelia's arms pinwheeled as she tried to gain her balance. Her eyes went wide with shock. The Reanimates wrapped their hands around her arms and legs, lifting her off the ground. She kicked her legs out, looking like she was crowd surfing.

Beckett wrapped his hand around my arm and yanked me to face him. "This is not who you are!"

"She took Zinnia from us. She deserves this!" I felt it in my bones. My friend was gone.

Grayson was by his side in an instant. "No, love, she doesn't. Stop this, now."

I couldn't stop, not now, not ever. Beckett took a step back from me. Blue smoke seeped from his hands.

"No." I shoved my fists into his chest, knocking him back. "She will suffer! We've lost everything—*everything*. My friend, our chance to kill Alataris . . . it's all gone now." My gaze locked onto Ophelia being hefted up and down as she fought to free herself. "She *has* to pay."

Beckett shook his head. "Not like this." Blue smoke shot from his hands anew.

I let my magic go wild. Purple sparks leapt across the floor, and my Reanimates hauled her toward a cell. I wanted them to throw her across the jail to hurt her the way she'd hurt all of us.

"Enough!" Beckett threw a wave of magic over us all.

My body jerked back, and I went flying across the room. When my feet touched the ground, I skidded back a couple feet until I bumped into the wall. Beckett shoved forward. His magic spilled over the floor, taking out my Reanimates one by one.

I shook my head and sucked in a deep breath as I staggered toward them. "I have to."

I needed revenge. I needed to not feel this gaping pit in my stomach. I needed . . . I fell forward and pressed my head into his chest. *I need Zinnia back.*

Beckett wrapped his hands around my shoulders and hugged me to him. Tears poured down my face, and racking sobs cut up my throat.

"She was my best friend."

"Shh." He tried to soothe me, but nothing he could say or do worked.

All at once, the fight left my body and was replaced with utter sadness. This time, I let go of my rage and allowed the heaving sobs to rack my chest. I didn't bother fighting the tears or the ball in my throat. I let the grief have me.

"That's it, Nova love. Let it go." Grayson brushed his hand down my arm. His touch was cool against my too hot skin. Even so, I found no comfort in any of it. Zinnia was gone.

I lifted my hand and commanded the Reanimates to drop Ophelia into the cell next to where Tuck had been kept. I peeked out from under Beckett's arms in time to see them lift her over their heads and drop her into the center of the cell. She landed in a heap on the hard stone, and a blank look came over her face. As the last zombie creature walked out, the cell door slid shut behind him.

Ophelia scrambled back into the corner and curled in on herself. She pulled her knees in toward her chest, and her whole body quivered. "I-I thought this would work. I thought I could save them all." She pressed her forehead to her knees and began to cry. "She was all I had left."

CHAPTER 3

BECKETT

The last of the Reanimates crawled back into the ground where they came from, leaving behind the upheaved rocks and dirt. I pulled my warlock magic back into my palms and gazed at the scene around me. Ophelia huddled in a ball in the corner of a cell, and Nova clung to me. Tucker held Zinnia in his burning arms. It was a slow fire, the kind that flickered like candlelight. It illuminated the cell with a warm, soft tone, a tone that was too peaceful for what had just happened here. My insides were balled into disgusted knots. I wanted to throw up and scream all at the same time. I'd thrown off my past and found a place here and a purpose. Now it was all gone. Alataris had won and hadn't even lifted a finger to do it.

My shirt was balled around Nova's fists as her tears

soaked through the material and fell onto my skin. I had yet to sleep and was still dressed in my tux from the night before. It was funny to think one night I was on such a high, ready to dance and have fun with my friends, and the next I was grieving for the loss of one of our own.

"Come on, just take a deep breath." I gently walked Nova back over to the bench, and we both sat, keeping watch over our grieving leader, Tucker.

His flames gently danced over both of them. His face was crumpled in agony, and his lips were pressed into a hard line as silent tears fell from his eyes. When he reached out toward her face, his hands shook uncontrollably. He brushed his fingers over her cheek and through her hair, smoothing the strands back. "You're not dead, Zin. I know you're not." He clutched her tighter. "I know you can hear me. Just open your eyes for me."

I didn't want to be here. I didn't want to watch him break into a million pieces. "Tuck, man, come on."

His head shot up, and when he looked at me, flames forked out from his eyes. "She . . . is . . . not . . . dead," he snapped, then turned back to her. With one shaking hand, he kept brushing her face and hair. With the other, he held her tight. "Are you, my Zin? No, you're going to be just fine. Aren't you?"

Tucker dropped to his knees with her in his arms. With his back to me, he huddled over, facing her. He bowed his head forward. "Please, Creator, don't take her from me. Not yet."

Tucker was *praying*. He was one of my best friends. I knew him well. And in that time, I'd never seen him pray, not once. But here he was huddled over Zinnia, praying for death to undo something that couldn't be taken back. She was gone. Her pale skin and the blue tinge to her lips were all signs. All hope was lost. Without her, there was no chance for any of us.

Tuck rocked her back and forth. "Please, please, please." He looked at the heavens. "I have never asked you for anything. Well, I'm asking now. Don't take her. It's not her time to go."

He looked back down at her chest. I knew he was willing her lungs to fill with air, trying with everything in him to force her to breathe.

Nova leaned away from my chest and swiped at her tears. "Tucker, don't."

He glanced over his shoulder at her. "Don't what? Don't pray that she's not dead? Don't feel like this is all my fault? Don't keep hoping that she'll come back to me?"

Nova shook her head and leaned back into me. I wrapped my arm around her shoulders and held her close, trying to comfort her. When I met Tuck's eyes, I didn't want to say it, didn't want to kill any hope he had. "Tuck, please."

He turned away from me and let his head slouch down and hugged her tighter. A gut-wrenching scream ripped from his lips. It was the scream of a man who'd lost everything that meant something to him. Flames erupted from his back and moved down his arms. They weren't the gentle flickering ones. No, this was a raging bonfire of turmoil. Burning embers floated from his skin. The flames moved over his arms in an array of blues and reds. Yet nothing else caught fire around him.

A banging sounded from just outside the door. The walls vibrated as if a battering ram were about to plow into the wooden door. Dust rained down from the ceiling, and tiny pebbles skidded across the floor. The door splintered in, sending shards of wood toward us. I threw my hand over Nova's face, covering her from the debris. My magic rose up, ready to protect them from whatever it was about to attack. Blue orbs spun around my fingers, ready to throw.

Kumi leapt through the opening, swishing her fluffy nine tails. Her black fur was sticking up across her shoulders, her ears were pressed back against her head, and a low growl rumbled deep in her chest.

The moment those violet eyes landed on Zinnia's

still form, Kumi's demeanor changed in an instant. She dropped down onto her stomach, and a whimpering cry filled the room. She belly-crawled across the floor toward Zinnia, all the while crying and moaning in pain. When she finally reached Zin, her body went limp, and she lay on her side directly across from Tucker. A low, heart-breaking howl filled the room. She pawed at the floor beside Zinnia and whimpered even louder. Tears the size of golf balls dripped from her eyes and rolled down her black fur, then smacked into the floor. It was her way of sobbing, and damn if it didn't break my heart all over again. I wanted to turn away. The overwhelming desire to leave the room filled me. At that moment, I wished I'd been one of the ones to get hurt in the fight the night before. But I couldn't leave. I had to stay here for them all . . . for her.

Tucker's body shook from head to toe, and his phoenix fire spread even farther down his back. The edge of the cot caught a flame, and I leapt up to pat it out. As I moved in closer, I felt it—a spark of magic. Not mine or Nova's or even Tucker's phoenix magic. No, this was something else, a pull like I'd only felt a few times. "Tuck!"

"Shut up, Beck. I'm not leaving." When he looked at me, his eyes were filled with embers. "I feel something. I swear it. I'm not crazy!"

"Don't leave. I believe you. Light up. Give her all you've got!" I dared not hope, but I had to know.

He tilted his head to the side. "What?"

"Light her up. NOW!"

Without hesitation, he wrapped his arms around her body and let his phoenix flames cover them both. The weird part was . . . Zinnia didn't burn.

CHAPTER 4

OPHELIA

I huddled in a ball in the corner of my cell with my arms around my knees. I pulled them in close to my chest. I wanted to stop shaking, to not show any kind of weakness around these people. Hell, they'd attacked me with Reanimates. I didn't ever want to see one of those zombie creatures again. After being raised in Alataris' court, I knew never to show fear or weakness, not now, not ever. But I couldn't stop the disgusted shudders from crawling up my spine. I thought being at Evermore Academy would be a new chance at life. But here I was locked in a room alone.

Just like home.

I'd let myself hope this experience would give me a place to belong, a purpose. I believed being with Zinnia and the rest of the queens would be good. I wanted to think I could make real friends, and maybe get closer to the sister I never knew I had, but always wanted. I'd been alone in the world all my life, and for the first time, I thought I might not be. I couldn't decide what was worse, never knowing happiness or knowing I'd ruined the only joy I'd ever felt. I wanted to be here with all of them, with her. In my gut, I knew this was where I fit and who I fit in with.

A deep ache in my heart took root, and I pressed one of my hands to my chest to try and rub it away. I shook my head. I refused to believe that potion wouldn't work. Tucker was free of his hex. Now all Zinnia had to do was wake up. She wasn't dead. If my sister was dead, I'd somehow feel it. No, in my heart I knew she wasn't gone. She couldn't be. The potion would work. I locked my eyes on her limp body and willed her to move with everything I had in me. I narrowed my eyes.

Breathe, damn it! I know you're still in there.

I would never hurt Zinnia. She was my family, the only living relative I had in this world aside from my loathsome father. The potion should've worked. Everyone should be alive and well. But everything went wrong, and now I was trapped in a cell.

My fourth birthday was the last time I cried. It was the day I learned my mother passed away. It'd been nearly twelve years since I dropped a single tear. Now the damn things wouldn't stop. And why the hell was my breathing so off? Was I bawling? Crap. I refocused my efforts and stared at her harder.

Come on, Zinnia, come on!

I ran the back of my hand over my eyes and cheeks. When it came back damp, I wrinkled my nose at it.

This can't be happening. That potion was perfect.

I made it myself. I checked it and double-checked it. I was trying to help them all, to save everyone. To prove myself to the crew, I took the chance, and I wanted them to trust me. I was here to get rid of my father once and for all. Instead, I ended up hurting the one person I could count on, the one person I needed in my life. Without her, I was alone in the world . . . my sister.

Across from me, Tucker held Zinnia in his arms. His flames were burning out of control, yet I felt a heavy magic in the air, a power I couldn't explain. But as the fire danced all over them, I found myself mesmerized by them. I saw figures and memories I wanted to bury deep in my head and never look at again. When they burned bright white and blue, I was captivated. Magic bloomed all around in an array of silver sparks, and exhaustion overcame me. I felt myself being lulled by the flames, watching them flicker in the dark basement. I didn't want to lose focus. If I kept my attention on Zinnia, I knew she'd wake up.

She has to wake up.

But the pull was too much, and I found myself tumbling down a rabbit hole of memories I didn't want to surface. One minute I was curled in on myself in the cell, and the next I was on a rocky cliff of a steaming river in the Peruvian Amazon.

Hot mist rose from between the rock as I tiptoed my way across them. Sweat beaded the back of my neck, and I was taking my time not to wake a sleeping two-headed serpent. Though I had on my hiking boots, my father still made me wear that black dress with white collar. My hair was braided in two pigtails down the sides of my head . . . because you treat me like I'm five years old still. *I needed to get out of here. Only yesterday I learned I had a sister, and now I was planning on getting to her.*

"Move your ass," my father snapped from behind me.

If you think it's so easy, why don't you come out here and do this? *I wanted to yell back at him, but I'd learned long ago not to talk back. Not unless I wanted a smack in the face or to be locked in my room. Which I didn't. I was going to escape him tonight to find my family, my real family.*

The serpent lay flat on the rocks, sunning itself. A stream of steaming water seeped from one of its heads, and cool water came from the other head. Its body was easily seventy feet long and as thick as a bus. I knew from my studies it struck with lightning speed and either of its heads could swallow me whole.

"Yes, Father."

"Get the damn flower. I can hear the Witch Court coming for it. This will be the last one and we will have it." Alataris kept a safe distance from where I was. He always kept a safe distance.

"Yes, I'm working on it, sir." I held my arms up as though I was balancing on a tightrope. I lifted my leg and leapt over the end of the snake's tail. My balance faltered, and I spun my arms to stop from falling back onto it.

"Ugh, stupid girl."

I could hear him pacing back and forth. He made no effort to keep quiet, no worry as to what would happen to me if he woke the sleeping beast. My foot slipped on a damp rock, and I stumbled forward. I pressed my hand to the ground, catching myself. The sharp rocks scratched at my palms. It was nothing compared to the injuries I'd received from him. I shifted my weight back and stood up straight. The Poppy Orchid we came here for only grew in one spot, but I was the only one here who could identify the right one. This particular species had a defense mechanism. Two buds always grew from each vine, but only one held the ingredient he was looking for. Why he needed it now was to lash out and hurt Zinnia, but I would do his bidding like I always did. Except this time things would go my way. If I could get this flower to her, to show her I wanted to start fresh, maybe she'd give me a chance. I hated every moment with him. My only consoling thought was it would all be over soon.

The flower was just on the edge of the waterfall. A field of them bloomed over the rocks, but the most potent one was closest to the edge. I walked over to it. I didn't want my father to see me pick this flower. I shifted my stance. I squatted low, giving my back to him. The sun beat down on my back as I reached out and plucked the flower with the deadly poppy seeds he wanted so badly. My gut warned me against something, but I didn't know what. My instincts had never let me down, and they wouldn't now. I shoved the flower down the sleeve of my dress. The thorns pinched at my skin, but I would suffer through it until I could run away and get it to Zinnia. I quickly pulled its twin and held it up in the air as I looked out over the beautiful Amazon.

The sky was so clear and blue. I could see the jungle for miles. While I held the flower in the air, I peeked over my shoulder at my father. "I got it."

In a puff of black smoke, he was by my side. I wanted to roll my eyes. If he could just float over here, why did he make me creep past a snake to do this?

Our features were only slightly similar. We both had shining pin-straight black hair and dark obsidian eyes. But that's where the similarities ended. My face was softer, heart-shaped, and his was long and oval. He was tall, gangly, and spider-like, with long arms and legs. I was shorter, petite, and all soft curves. I liked to think I favored my mother more than him, but my memories of her were hazy at best.

"I'll take that." He snatched the flower out of my hand and brought it to his nose. "So beautiful."

I nodded at him. "Can we go now?"

"We?" He shook his head and tsked. "No, not we, my darling."

"Father wha—"

He shoved his hands into my shoulders, knocking me backward. I reached out for his hand, but he stepped away. A broad smile spread across his lips.

My body tipped back, and I spun my arms, trying to find my balance. It was too late. My body twisted, and my stomach dropped down to my toes. A scream ripped from my throat as I fell over the edge of the waterfall. My life flashed before my eyes, and all I saw was my room, which was more like a cell, and the treachery in my father's eyes.

At the last second, I caught myself by the tips of my fingers on the edge of the rocks. I kicked my legs, trying to boost myself up and get a better grip. "Father, help me."

He leaned over the side of the waterfall, gazing down his nose at me. His boots were barely an inch away from my fingers. "Why?"

I would've liked to be surprised at that moment, but I wasn't. I let my face fall into the cold calm I always used when dealing with him. Even though my heart was pounding, cold sweat broke out over my body and my fingers tingled painfully as I gripped the edge with everything I had. "What do you mean, why? I'm your daughter."

He canted his head to the side. "And a queen."

"Pull me up . . ." I hesitated. I never begged my father for anything. "Please."

"Please?" He threw his head back, laughing. "The prophecy says it takes five queens to be rid of me. Well, if there aren't five queens, then I live to fight another day."

"I'm your blood!" I held on by two fingers.

"Pity, isn't it?" A flame danced down his arm and up toward his fingertips. He turned his hand and let the sparks drop onto the vines running over the rocky face.

"No, please don't." I looked down the waterfall. Jagged rocks forked out between the misting pool.

But when a slow smile spread across his face, I knew I was doomed. It was the same face I'd seen each time he sucked the magic and soul out of someone to create a Thrall or each time he would go in for the kill. His black eyes would go vacant, and that smile would spread from ear to ear as if the monster within had taken over. The vines caught fire, and flames began to lick the sky behind him. The snake rose up to tower over him, yet it didn't see him. It only had eyes for me. All four of those eyes focused . . . only . . . on . . . me. I shoved down my panic, but I couldn't control my heart from racing.

I swallowed around the ball in my throat and mumbled under my breath. "Plummeting, falling I shall not do. Defying gravity is what must come true. Let the eye see that which is false and keep me safe until hope is no longer lost. Sky above, grant me wings. Ground below, protect me from all harmful things."

Just as my father lifted his foot to stomp down on my fingers, I let go and watched as the flames behind him devoured the remaining flowers I knew Zinnia was looking for. But I had the last one, the one that would earn her trust in me. The mist of the waterfall swallowed me from his sight, but the second he could no longer see me, my free fall changed to a slow drift toward the ground. The snake dove over the edge after me. Its two heads hissed simultaneously. Once my feet touched the ground, I didn't hesitate to dart into the thick woods. The snake hit the pool at the bottom of the waterfall with a resounding splash. Drops of water fell over my face and clothing. Under the cover of the lush jungle, I gazed up, watching those flames burn a bright red, killing the last of the flowers. Every flame burned into my memories. The same memories I fought back with everything I had.

Now all I would do was get to my sister . . . my family.

CHAPTER 5

"I can't help but think she's going to do the worst to save him. This hex is deadly, Matteaus." For more than half my life, I'd been preparing to be the mentor of the queens and knights. It killed me to stand by and merely guide them and not step in myself, but the prophecy was specific. Mentors were just that—a guiding hand not meant to fight themselves. There were so many times I wished I could fight or go along on a mission. It was forbidden. All I could do was study all possible situations and advise them. But nothing could've prepared me for this, for my lead knight to be under a hex and one of my queens going out of her mind to save him.

"That hex is deadly. But what can we do?" Matteaus

shook his head. "You know I've been tempted to just kill him myself."

"Haven't we all. But you know the rules must be followed. It's their destiny. This is only one battle among many to come for them." I stood at barely five feet tall. On a good day, I felt short. Next to Matteaus' hulking stature, I felt downright childlike. He was well over six feet tall and tipping the scales at least at 280 pounds of hard muscle. A leather belt hung loosely around his hips, holding a sword longer than my upper body. Loose black leather pants covered his legs, and a white V-neck T-shirt barely hid the cords of muscles of his upper body. He held his arm up, motioning for me to walk with him across the courtyard.

I took a step out through the archway and began walking beside him. All evidence of the dance from the night before was gone. Cool fall wind swept through the center of the school, blowing papers right out of students' hands and sending a small chill over my skin.

Winter will be here soon.

The hum of the trickling water fountain echoed all around. Students lounged in the grass and by the side of the fountain. The sun had just barely set, and a faint purplish glow still clung to the sky. Pixies fluttered around, emitting golden and silver dust in their wake. Light laughter drifted from the other students. They were so carefree, much freer than my knights and queens. I wished they had a chance to be normal sixteen and seventeen-year-olds, to know what it was like to only worry about their schooling. Instead, they were fighting for their lives against an evil king three times their age and skill level.

I sucked in a deep breath. "I suspect Zinnia has a plan, but I need to find out what it is before she hurts herself or someone else. So many of our attempts to heal him have failed. I fear she's going to do something drastic."

A deep chuckle rumbled in his chest. "I hate to break it to you, but when teenagers with an immense amount of power are involved, it's always drastic. I will say this: it is the first time I feel like the queens who ascended might have a chance against Alataris. And now that Ophelia is here, things are looking up."

"I wish that were true. But we really have no idea why she is here and if it will be to our benefit. Alataris is known for being underhanded. She could be here to ensure something awful happens." The moment I laid eyes on Ophelia, I wanted to believe she was on our side. But, how could I?

He paused mid-step and met my gaze. "Like what?"

I clutched the books I held closer to my chest. "The prophecy states it will take the power of all five queens to defeat Alataris. If only one of them fell, it would end this cycle and he would be safe for at least another sixteen years, possibly more. If I were thinking like him, I would take one of them out as soon as possible, and what better way to do it than to get at them from the inside?"

"So, are you saying you want to send Ophelia packing?" He crossed his arms over his chest. The enormous black wings on his back trembled slightly, and feathers fell to the ground at his feet.

I pushed my glasses farther up my nose. "No, I think she's here for a reason. I just don't know what it is, but we have to figure it out soon."

Matteaus reached out and placed his hand on my shoulder. "Maybe she's here to actually help."

"I'd like to believe that. I really would. But I've spent years reading the histories of past battles of the queens who didn't survive, and I know there isn't one line he wouldn't cross. Even if it means using his own daughter to do his dirty work."

"I agree with you. But, Niche, there's one thing I think you always need to have."

I sucked in a deep breath. "What's that?"

He motioned for us to continue along our way. "Hope. We have to have hope that this time will be different. Otherwise, what is the point of trying?"

"I do have hope, but it's a cautious hope. I can't lie. I'm truly concerned about Ophelia's motives, and what about Zinnia? She seems willing to go to extreme lengths for Tucker."

"Ah." A wistful smile played on his lips. "But what wouldn't we do for young love?"

I froze. Had I been so blind? "What do you mean?"

He pointed to the books in my hand. "Your nose couldn't have been buried that deep in a book not to realize their connection."

I shook my head, and tendrils of my fire engine red hair fell into my face. "It is forbidden."

"Sometimes the forbidden fruit is the sweetest." He rubbed his thumb over his bottom lip. "Something I know all too well."

My pulse quickened. "Not in this case. They'll prize each other above everyone else. Two cycles ago, there was a pairing within the queens and knights. They all died, Matteaus, but not before Alataris made them choose between each other and the rest of their team. And they all died horribly from it. No, Tuck will have to be sent back to Cindelore to take his place as prince of the Phoenix clan."

"Niche, he's trained his whole life for this position. Do you really think he knows any other way of life? The boy is a warrior through and through if ever I saw one.

Honestly, if he survives this, the thought had crossed my mind to employ him myself once he gets older. You know we could use his help in the grand scheme."

Before I could say anything else, the world trembled under my feet, forcing me to lose my balance. My books toppled from my hands and fell to the ground. Matteaus' warm hand wrapped around my arm and steadied me. I looked around at the rest of the students toppling over. "What's happening?"

Streams of silver magic shot up from the ground like geysers. Rocks and dirt flew in all different directions. Students screamed and ran for cover. Dust rained down on the courtyard as Zinnia's magic snaked out like the legs of Kraken. One by one, those silver streams of magic lashed around any magical living thing and held on. When my gaze met Matteaus' turbulent sea blue eyes, his face was a mirror of my own panic.

I spun in a circle, watching as student after student fell under the onslaught of her power. "My God. It's her . . . Zinnia."

His grip tightened around my arm. "We have to find her before her magic kills them all."

In the corner of the courtyard, Tabi, our Queen of Elements, and Serrina, our Queen of Desires, appeared. They'd just emerged from the infirmary and were stepping into the courtyard when the world went crazy.

I cupped my hands around my mouth, screaming at them. "Get out. Run!"

As the words flew from my mouth, two snake-like streams slammed into their chests. I turned to go to them, but Matteaus caught me around the waist. "No. The only way this will stop is if we find Zinnia."

The wind kicked up, sending miniature cyclones skidding through the courtyard. Matteaus' wings sprang from his back. "Get to her. I have to help here."

He shoved me under one of the archways where students huddled for cover. The mini tornado picked up a small boy and sent him flying in the opposite direction. Matteaus shot off the ground and caught him in midair. Just as fast as the tornados started, they suddenly stopped, and there was nothing but dead silence.

I lumbered to my feet, watching as her magic seeped across the ground like fog. Then drop by drop, it rose up like rain in reverse. The lanterns around the courtyard flared, sending the flames three feet high. Wild screams filled the air as the fountain cracked in half, sending water erupting from the ground.

"What do you people have against my fountain?" Matteaus growled as he picked up two more students and tossed them over his shoulder to carry them to safety.

I crept to the next column toward a younger witch who lay unconscious. *Please let her be alive.* I pressed my fingers to the side of her neck.

Matteaus dropped down beside me. "Is she . . .?"

"Not dead. Just sleeping, I think." Her pulse was calm and steady. Her breath came in deep, even puffs.

"Sleeping? What the hell is going on?" He glanced around as people dropped to the soaking ground, all seeming to fall asleep on the spot.

"I think she's draining their powers. It won't kill them. They'll replenish eventually. I think we've been lucky so far. Someone could die." Just then, the water from the fountain went still. Everything froze, and every drop pulled together into a river that flowed down one specific hallway. I pointed toward it. "Follow that river!"

Matteaus grabbed my arm and hauled me to my feet. "Let's go!"

I tried to keep up with him as best as I could. He was a fallen angel, and I was a mere witch. Silver streams of magic followed behind us as though chasing me. I pumped my arms and ran faster. Lines of her magic rose up around me like bars on a jail cell. My heart hammered in my chest, and I sucked in deep breaths. "Matteaus!"

He turned back and reached his hand out to grab me. That's when I felt it slam into my chest and fork out through my veins. Her magic punched me in the stomach, knocking the wind from my lungs. The magic drained from my body, leaving exhaustion in its place. My knees gave out, and my face fell toward the ground. Matteaus swept his arm out and caught me just before I smacked into the hard-stone ground.

Her magic hovered over him like a dome, never seeking or taking. He cradled me against his chest. "You okay?"

My eyelids were so heavy I could barely keep them open. "Find her."

He pressed his lips into a hard line. "I will."

"Stop her." My eyelids fluttered, and then there was nothing but blackness.

CHAPTER 6

OPHELIA

A downpour of ice-cold water dropped on me as if someone dumped a bucket over my head. I sucked in a shocked breath and shoved my inky hair out of my face. All thoughts of my homicidal father were forgotten as I was brought back to the present. Water flooded into the room from the cracks in the walls and rose higher with each passing second. My clothes were sopping wet and clung to my body. I trudged through thigh-high water toward the cell bars. Silver magic swirled around Zinnia in a tornado of fire and magic. Zinnia hovered just over Tuck's head, yet he kept his arms reaching up toward her, and his phoenix blaze continued even with the water pouring in. A wall of her magic kept the water from seeping out of the open doorway. We were fish in a bowl about to spill over.

I wrapped my hands around the frigid metal bars. "Zinnia! You have to wake up!"

Beckett and Grayson stood on either side of Nova, holding her limp body above the rising tide. Though Zinnia's magic was latched into all their chests, they fought to keep their eyelids open. Even now they swayed on their feet. If they passed out, nothing would stop them from drowning. Kumi sloshed back and forth like a sailboat in a hurricane.

A loud pounding sounded just outside her wall of magic. "Ophelia!"

My heart skyrocketed at the sound of the familiar voice. "Cross?"

"Are you okay? All hell is breaking loose out here."

I glanced around at the rising water, the burning fire, and everyone struggling not to pass out and drown. "Um, I'm not really sure." I gripped the bars tighter to hold myself in place.

"I'm coming! Just hold on. Make sure everyone is clear of this wall thing."

"What?" Between the roaring of the trickling water and the crackling flames, it was difficult to hear what he was saying.

A hole burned through the center of the silver wall. Smoky burgundy warlock magic seeped through it like burning embers. Cracks forked across the silvery wall like glass about to shatter. I buried my face in the crook of my arm to protect it from debris. BOOM! The wall gave way and the water rushed out the open door. It swept my feet out from under me. Kumi lost her footing and slid out the door right past Cross. I clung to the bars to stop from falling to the ground. Across from me, Grayson, Beckett, and Nova fell to the rushing tide and skidded over the floor and into the wall next to the door, where they all lay unconscious. The steady rise and fall of their chests told me they were alive. But for how long?

Cross stormed into the room like an avenging angel. His midnight hair hung in damp tatters down the sides of his face, and in the light of Tucker's flames, his gold eyes were tiger-like. He held his hand up, shielding his eyes from the inferno that Tuck and Zinnia had created.

When his narrowed gaze roamed over me, he pressed his lips into a thin line. "They locked you up?"

I nodded and swallowed around the ball in my throat. "Yeah."

He turned his scrutiny on the rest of the crew. Burgundy smoke drifted from his palms. The muscle in his jaw flexed as he gritted his teeth. "How . . . could . . . they?"

"Cross!" I reached my hand through the bars. "Please just get me out of here."

"They should pay." His eyes glowed bright gold, and his power seeped from his hands onto the damp floor. I didn't want him to attack them—not yet, anyway. I could feel Zinnia's power, knew she would wake at any second. They all needed to see I saved her, that I saved Tuck and they could trust me.

I shook my head. "No, leave them."

His muscles looked impossibly bigger under the black long-sleeved T-shirt that clung to his body. He stood rigid, looking back and forth between them and me. He hesitated a moment before marching over to the cell. He placed his hands over mine. "You're freezing. Let's get you out of here."

I wanted to nod in agreement, but my eyes were drawn back toward Zinnia. The ball of fire swirling around her grew brighter, so bright I had to turn my face away but didn't. Heat licked at my skin, so hot my clothing started to dry. I squinted against the light.

Zinnia threw her hands up as though she were swimming backward, and her eyes flashed wide-open. Locks of her midnight hair danced with flames and silver magic. "Tuck?"

My heart rate skyrocketed, and my body thrummed tight with excited tension. Tuck's eyes flashed wide, and his flames extinguished in an instant. Zinnia dropped from her floating position and fell into Tuck's waiting arms. He tumbled down to the ground, looking more exhausted than I'd ever seen him. Yet he cradled Zinnia in his arms as he sat on the ground.

She threw her arms around his neck and pulled him in closer to her. "You're okay?"

"Me?" He tipped his head back and met her gaze, then brushed the hair from her face. Tears swam in his eyes. "You died, Zinnia. Don't ever do that to me again. Do you hear me?"

Zinnia leaned into his chest. "I wasn't really dead, you know?"

A single tear rolled down the side of his cheek, and he sniffled. "But you were."

She shook her head. "But the potion—"

"Killed you. I don't know how you're here now with me, but it's a miracle." He pressed his forehead to hers, then cupped her cheek.

When their lips met, Zinnia's eyes widened, and she drew back. "Tuck, people will see."

"Let them." He pressed his lips to hers once more. He wound his arms tight around her body and squeezed her close.

I wanted to look away, to give them the privacy they deserved, but I couldn't take my eyes off my sister. She was alive and well. "See? I told you all it would work!"

Zinnia's head snapped away from Tuck's. Her brow furrowed. "O, what the hell are you doing in a cell?"

I looked down at Cross' hands over mine, then back up at him. "Oh, um." I pulled my hands out from under his and moved to stand in front of the door. "We had a misunderstanding."

She moved to climb off of Tuck's lap, but he tightened his arm around her.

"Don't get up yet."

"I have to." She scrambled off him toward the door. Tiny flames danced in her hair and fell off her as she approached me.

"Um, Zin, you're on fire." I pointed to the sparks flying off her shoulder.

Zinnia's eyes widened as she smacked her hands over her body and patted them out. "What the hell happened?"

Tuck was by her side in an instant, patting the smoking flames out of her hair. "I told you." He swallowed audibly, and his breath hitched. "You died."

"Yeah, but just for like a second, right?" She looked from me at Tuck and back again.

I shook my head. "Not just for a second. It was a lot longer than a second." I bit my bottom lip. "I must've done something wrong."

Zinnia reached through the bars and placed her

hands over mine. "No, I'm here. Tuck's hex has been lifted. You saved us."

Tuck placed his hand on her shoulder. "Zinnia, I wouldn't say that. You were gone, and somehow your magic saved you. It brought you back. If it wasn't for that . . ."

"You don't know if that's true." I pulled my hands out from under Zinnia's and put them on my hips. "It could've been her magic that interfered with the potion."

"Hold up a second." She turned to stand between the two of us as if I wasn't still behind bars. "So, I was actually dead and came back, they locked you in a cell for my death, and now everything is fine?"

Matteaus lumbered in through the broken door. He hunched over, sucking in deep breaths. When he looked at me through narrowed eyes and turned that angry gaze on Zinnia, I knew we were in trouble. "NO! Everything is not fine!"

CHAPTER 7

ZINNIA

Matteaus stood to his full towering height and pointed his finger at me. "You. Here. Now."

Shiiiiiitttt. I backed away from the cell where Ophelia stood and took a step toward Matteaus. My body hummed with energy, both foreign and familiar.

What happened to me?

Magic flowed through my veins so strong I could almost taste it. I looked down at my hands just as purple sparks fired from my fingertips into the ground. Skeletal hands shot up from the ground and latched onto Matteaus' boots. He narrowed his eyes, and a growl rumbled in his chest as he kicked his legs out, shattering the hands trying to hold him.

I shook my head. "I didn't do it."

"Didn't you?" He stepped over the shattered bones

and into the dungeon. When he crossed his arms over his chest and looked around the room, I knew I was up shit creek. Puddles of water remained around the room. Two deep footprints were sunk into the middle of the floor surrounded by scorch marks. Craters of upended stone and dirt were scattered around, along with rotting limbs. Grayson, Beckett, and Nova all lay passed out on the floor looking like they'd fallen asleep right where they dropped.

Cross folded his arms over his chest and stared at me with murder in his eyes. It was a drastic change from the boy who'd come to the door to save me from going to the dance alone. "Oh yeah, she did it."

Ophelia rattled the bars behind me. "Shut up, Cross."

He pressed his lips together and didn't say another word. Yet he still looked at me like I'd destroyed his whole world. I swallowed around the nervous ball in my throat. A hiccup escaped my lips, and bubbles drifted from the top of my head and floated around me in a glassy array.

I held my hands up and let them pop on my fingertips. "What the hell?"

"That's exactly what this is—hell." Matteaus sucked in a deep breath. "Do you idiots have any idea what you've done? The entire school has been drained of their magic and they're passed out sleeping where they fell. The dungeon is destroyed—"

At that exact second, Kumi sprinted back into the room and reared up on her hind legs and pushed both of her paws right into my chest. I tipped backward, about to land flat on my back, but instead I gracefully rolled and landed in a crouch. My nails extended into long black talons, and an involuntary hiss escaped my lips.

What the . . .? Zinnia! It's me, Kumi! Her words drifted through my mind.

I shook my head and slowly rose to my feet. I studied my black talons as they slid back into my hands and transformed into my normal fingernails. *I know it's you.* "What's happening to me?"

"That's what I'm saying." Matteaus put his hands on his hips. "You siphoned the magic from the entire school!"

I pressed my hand over my mouth. "I did what?"

"And this"—he motioned toward me—"is magic overload escaping you any way it can. I'm surprised you haven't exploded yet. And to top it all off, you broke my fountain—again!"

I pressed my hands to my chest as my heart rate skyrocketed. "I'm going to explode?" I didn't feel like I was going to. In fact, I never felt better. I had energy,

Tuck was healed, and even though Ophelia was in a cell, she was still here. She helped save us all.

Tucker moved to stand next to me. "What do we have to do? I can't . . ." He swallowed hard. "I can't let anything happen to her."

I'd never seen Tuck so shaken. His skin was pale, and his honey eyes were jumping all around the room. He shifted from one foot to the other, all the while moving closer to me. I took a small step farther away from him. I wasn't sure what happened after I took the potion up until now, but something had shifted in him. He wasn't afraid to be close to me in front of others. Hell, he kissed me in front of Ophelia and Cross.

Matteaus looked him up and down, then sighed. "The only thing I can think of is for her to give back all the power she took."

"But will that . . . will it hurt her?" Whatever space I got from taking that small step away from him he took back by moving closer to me once more. His chest was now touching my back. I felt his racing heart through my shirt and the tremors rocking his body.

Matteaus shook his head. "I don't know, but we can't let all the students be in a coma because she siphoned all their power off."

"Guys, I feel fine." I looked up at Tucker. "I can do this."

He placed a hand on my shoulder. Heat radiated through my shirt and into my skin. My phoenix was warm, so very warm. He pressed his fingers into me. "Okay, but I'm staying with you the whole time."

"Me too," Ophelia called from her cell. "Someone has to watch your ass."

Tucker snarled, "Haven't you done enough?"

I jabbed my elbow back into his stomach. "I trust Ophelia."

"That makes one of us." He huffed.

"I'm fine. I swear. She helped us more than you know." In fact, I felt great. I couldn't go into details in front of Matteaus, but the second I was alone with Tuck, I would explain everything from start to finish. There were so many secrets I had to tell him. Ophelia was my sister. Which if I compared it to who my father was, wasn't so bad. He had to know it all. But not in front of the headmaster.

Matteaus sighed. "Zinnia?"

Is he reading my mind? I fought the balls of nerves in my stomach. "Yes?" *I might puke.*

He pointed to where Tuck's hand rested on my shoulder. "You're on fire."

As I walked up the stairs and out of the dungeon, cool air swept through the hall leading to the courtyard. Evermore always had a constant buzz of activity about it, but now only eerie silence greeted me. Even the busy pixies looked like they dropped from midair and fell into a deep sleep. I tiptoed over each of them, taking care not to crush one. Tucker held one of my hands and helped me climb over a puppy pile of sleeping students. As I moved closer to the center of the school, I could feel their powers moving inside of me, each of them pulling me in different directions to let them out.

My eyes widened. "I did all this?"

Matteaus walked up beside me and nodded. "I don't know what happened in that dungeon, but I do know you are a very powerful witch, Zinnia. Now the question is, how are you going to use that power?" He motioned to the bodies lying everywhere. "Because you're capable of this. And much worse."

What was he saying? That one day I'd turn into my father? I would never.

I ground my teeth together. "This was an accident."

"Which is why I'm not tossing you out on your ass right now. You're young and learning your powers, but this, my dear, is very dangerous. We're lucky no one was killed. Now it's up to you to decide how to use what you've got. Will you rule like Alataris, or is this life enough for you?"

"I will never be like him." This was an accident. The guilt sat heavy in my stomach, slowly eating at me. As I came closer to the courtyard, I saw a lock of fire engine red hair lying across the cold ground. "Niche, no."

I let go of Tucker's hand and rushed to her side. I dropped down to my knees and hovered over her sleeping body. "Oh God, Niche, I'm so sorry." I brushed a lock of her hair off her forehead. "I-I didn't know this would happen. I swear."

Tucker squatted down next to me. Those dark auburn locks fell across his forehead into his honey eyes. Even after he brushed them back, they just fell back into place. He ran his hand in rhythmic circles over my back. "We know. You just have to make it right now."

I nodded up at him with my determination flowing through me. "Okay, let's do this."

Tuck held his hand out to me, and I took it. His lips pulled up in a half smile. "Then here we go."

We walked hand in hand toward the center of the courtyard. Cool air seeped into my skin, and I spun in the small circle, breathing in the night air. I looked at the sky, wishing I could see the stars past the lights of the New York skyline.

"All you have to do is take a deep breath and release

what you can." Tucker stepped back from me. "But not too much, okay?"

I held my hands up, gathering my magic in my palms. Silver sparkles danced over my skin. Flames joined in with the sparkles, and a smile tugged at my lips. *My Phoenix.*

Tucker stood next to Matteaus, bouncing on the balls of his feet. "I mean it, Zin. Nothing more than you can afford to give."

I wanted to reassure him, but I didn't know how much I had to give or what kind of magic I had left over. I wanted to give everyone everything I took from them. I didn't mean to, yet it happened. Now I had to correct it.

I let my powers bloom from my palms. Silver sparks floated up from my hands and an array of colorful magic mixed with mine. Reds, yellows, greens, and purples all joined my silver. Bubbles floated and popped around me. I lifted my arms, pushing it all up toward the sky. A dome of magic spread over the courtyard. Sweat beaded my brow, and I felt the weight of all the magic I was carrying. My arms shook, yet I tried to push the dome up higher.

"Zinnia, enough." Tucker took a step toward me.

Matteaus' arm snapped across Tuck's chest. He pulled him back. "She is a queen, so you have to let her do this. Not just for the students of the Academy, but for herself as well. Her powers are growing. Let them."

When my eyes met Tucker's, he tilted his head to the side. His face fell into a mask of seriousness while the muscle in his jaw ticked with tension. He wasn't the confident phoenix shifter I'd known all this time. Now he was on edge, nervous even. Whatever happened down in that dungeon affected him, and not in a good way.

"Focus. The Academy is counting on you." Matteaus gave me a nod of confidence.

If I kept looking at Tuck, I would never be able to do this. I turned my gaze to the sky and the dome of magic spreading over the entire school. It rose up like a nuclear cloud, a swirling ball of multicolored magic. The muscles in my arms weighed down with fatigue, and I pushed my magic even harder. When it peeked over the top of the school, I threw my arms out, letting it all go. Magic rained down on the school in a slow fall, like quiet snow in the middle of the night. Sparkles caught in my hair and over my clothing. It fell into Tucker's tasseled auburn locks, and for a moment, all I could see was him. We were the only two people standing in a snow-covered winter mountain with not a care in the world.

The snowy magic drifted over the sleeping students.

One by one, their eyes fluttered open, and they looked around, asking each other what happened.

Matteaus strolled up to me with a wide smile spread across his face. The falling magic didn't touch him. It fell around him like he had a protective barrier over his entire body. "You did it."

Exhaustion hit me like a ton of bricks, and I yawned. "I'm sorry I knocked out the whole school."

Matteaus placed one hand on my shoulder and his other on Tuck's. "Look, I'm not going to pretend to know what happened tonight. But I do know a few things about forbidden love. Let's just say my past hasn't exactly been pristine even after we fell. But you both have to know what happened here tonight can never happen again." He motioned between the two of us. "And this, whatever it is, keep it under wraps for a while longer. We wouldn't want our phoenix getting shipped off, would we?"

"No." I shook my head. I couldn't be here without Tuck. Now more than ever I needed him by my side. "We'll keep it under wraps until things are more *settled*."

Tucker gave me a sharp look then hesitated for only a moment before he nodded. "Very well."

"Good. Now I think both of you should go and get some rest. You're going to have a lot to deal with tomorrow." He patted me on the shoulder, then walked toward a group of students milling around the courtyard looking like they needed to go back to sleep. Matteaus cupped his hands around his mouth and yelled, "Everyone to their dormitories. Class resumes in two days' time. Rest and recuperate tomorrow."

A couple of halfhearted cheers came from the exhausted students. They all shuffled toward their dorm rooms.

Tuck ran his fingers down my arm, leaving a scorching trail of heat down my skin as he wrapped my hand in his. "Let's go get some rest."

After everything we'd been through, all I wanted to do was fall into a warm, cushy bed and not wake for a few days. But there were things I had to tell him, things that needed to be said. "Okay, but first there's something we need to do."

CHAPTER 8

ZINNIA

Tuck's room was right next mine and nearly a mirror of everything I had. A full-size bed sat up against one wall, with a wooden desk directly across from it on the other wall. Niche and Matteaus had put him next door to me because he was the lead knight in our crew, my protector. They wanted him near me in case something happened. I wanted him near me because he was my soul mate, my everything. Our relationship was forbidden, and yet here we were lying in his bed facing each other but not touching. Electricity pulsed between us, and I wanted to scoot closer to him, to press my body against his and feel he was okay. The whole time we'd been together, his eyes hadn't flickered to black once. The hex was indeed dead and gone. My plan had worked.

Tuck reached out a shaking hand and grabbed a lock of my hair and wound it between his fingers, toying with my wild waves. "I thought I lost you." His voice was low, and the pain in it mirrored the aching in my chest.

"But you didn't." I didn't dare move. If I did, he might send me back to my room, and I couldn't bear to be without him tonight. "I thought I lost *you*."

He squeezed his eyes shut and sighed. "Zinnia, if something happens to me, you have to let me go. You're more important to the world than a single knight. You're a queen, a siphon witch, and the others need you."

I shook my head. "I wouldn't be any good to anyone without you."

He dropped the lock of my hair and shifted closer to me. Our bodies still weren't touching, but I could feel the heat rolling off of him. When his eyes met mine, his gaze turned to liquid honey. "I understand, but where do we go from here? I . . . I . . ." His breath hitched. "I hurt you, Zinnia. I wanted to stop, but I lost control of myself. I couldn't bear it if something happened to you. I'm so sorry. I would never—"

"Tuck, I know you would never hurt me like that. You were under Alataris' hex. It wasn't you. It was him. He's the one who hurt me, not you." The sheets rustled under me as I got even closer to him. "Tuck, there's something I have to tell you."

We were soul mates. There could be no secrets between us, and I'd been carrying around the darkest secret of all for long enough. Would he kick me out? Reject me now? Not even I could accept the parts of myself that came from my father. How could I expect Tuck to accept them when I myself resented everything about Alataris?

"Zinnia?" He brushed his fingers down my cheek. "You can tell me anything."

I swallowed down my nerves and sucked in a deep breath. "Alataris is . . . well, he's, um . . . he's kind of . . . ugh, I don't know why this is so hard to say. He's my—"

"He's your father." Tuck finished the sentence I couldn't bear to utter.

My mouth dropped open into a little O. "How'd you know?"

"When he hexed me, I saw things, heard things I didn't know were true. But lying here with you now, seeing you struggle with this, I know it's true." He sank lower into the pillow and pulled the blanket up higher over my shoulder.

I lay there, waiting for him to say something more, to say he was okay with it. Or to reaffirm that he accepted me no matter who my shitty father was. But he didn't say anything. I couldn't sit here and wait for him to break my heart, to say there was no trust between us. I threw the blanket back and stood up. "I'm sorry. I have to go."

The moment my feet touched the cold floor, Tuck reached out and grabbed my hand, then pulled me back into bed. "Where are you going?"

I sat back down on the bed with my feet still touching the ground. "Away from here. Look, he's my father, and there's nothing I can do about it. But I don't want to sit here and know that you can't handle it. That you can't trust me."

Tucker crawled over to me and wrapped his arm around my waist and lifted me up to gently lay me back on his pillows. The side of my body was pressed up against his. Heat pooled in my stomach, and I wanted to be closer to him, so much closer. He rested his head on his hand and leaned over me. "I trust you. Hell, you gave your life for me. I don't give a shit who your father is. Or your sister, for that matter. Although I might avoid any future family dinners. I don't care about any of that." He swallowed. "Because I love you."

My heart slammed into overdrive. It hummed in my ears, and I sucked in a shocked breath. I didn't expect *I love you.* An involuntary smile pulled at my mouth. His tongue darted over his lips, and he plucked up a lock of my hair and started playing with it once more.

"I know I've said and done things to hurt you in the past, but aside from the hex, I did those things to protect you. It turns out you're the one who saved me. Zin, you don't have to say it ba—"

"I love you too!" The words rushed out of my mouth before I could stop them. Hell, I didn't want to stop them. I loved Tuck more than anything. We both nearly died for each other. Soul mates or not, we loved each other. This wasn't some mean twist of fate. This was destiny. We were meant to be. The mark on my wrist didn't have to tell me that. Everything about Tuck and me made sense.

His face turned up into a warm smile. "You love me?" Tiny flames danced through the tips of his hair and across his arms.

I put my hand over one of them, and it rolled over my skin like a drop of water. "Of course I do. Are you sure you love me? Even with all my crazy family drama?"

A light chuckle vibrated deep in his chest. "My family isn't exactly picture-perfect. We will get through this together."

For the first time since I'd gotten to Evermore Academy, Tuck and I were on the same page, and it felt amazing. I beamed up at him as I lifted my hand and wound in my fingers through his tousled dark auburn hair and tugged him closer. When his lips met mine, electricity shot through my veins, and there it was—that connection I craved only from him. I pressed my fingers into his shoulder and pulled him closer to me. Our tongues wound together, and his clean, minty taste invaded my senses. Heat bloomed over my body, and I needed him closer. *Much closer.*

I scooted toward him, and he rolled on top of me. I parted my thighs and let his body press up against mine. My legs tangled with his, and I pulled him tighter to me. I ran my hands down his back. His muscles rippled under my touch as I reached for the hem of his shirt. I twisted my fingers into the bottom of his shirt and ripped it up over his head. My gaze was drawn down to his tan skin and toned body. His skin was hot to the touch, and I wanted more. His lips slammed against mine, and I wrapped my arms around him. His hands slid over my stomach and farther up my shirt.

He paused and met my eye. "Is this okay?"

A flutter of nerves quivered deep in my stomach. But this was Tuck, my soul mate, my everything. We belonged together. I knew it in my heart. I nodded up at him, then reached down and tugged my shirt up over my head.

"Yeah, I'm very sure." I pressed my hand to his cheek. "It's always been you for me. I really do love you, Tuck."

"I love you too. Zin, just please promise me you won't ever be that reckless with your life again. I can't . . ." He sucked in a shuddering breath and pressed his fingers into my skin. "I can't live in a world where you don't exist."

His eyes were molten, and I knew he meant every word he said. "Then you know why I had to take the potion."

"I know." He pressed his lips to mine once more, and my body went wild under the feel of his hands on me. I reached down and popped the button on the top of my jeans. Yesterday, we'd nearly lost each other. Today, I had him in my arms and wasn't going to let go. As he slid my pants down my legs, I knew this was meant to be.

CHAPTER 9

ZINNIA

My body ached in all the right places as I lay pressed up against Tuck's side. My clothing was strewn about the room. The early morning sun peeked in through the windows, and Tuck's warmth seeped into my body. I ran my fingertips over the side of that wicked phoenix tattoo. The muscles under it rose up to meet my touch. Tuck slept by my side. His breaths were deep and even. It was the first moment of calm we'd had in weeks. I didn't want it to end. Try as I might, there was nothing I could do to stop from grinning like the Cheshire cat.

With his eyes closed and his face completely relaxed, I lay there watching him sleep. We'd solidified our relationship throughout the night, and I felt utterly complete with him. I wound my fingers in between his and looked at our matching soul mate marks. The continuous connecting infinity marks surrounded our wrists. Mine was thin and delicate. Tuck's was thicker and covered more of his skin. Tiny pearl colors swirled within each of the circles in the infinity signs. A calming warmth spread from the soul mate mark up my arm.

A smirk tugged at his lips, and his eyes blinked open slowly. "Hi."

"Hey."

He turned to face me and ran his fingers down my cheek. "Are you okay?"

"A little sore, but I'm good. Last night was more than I could've hoped for." I wanted to snuggle in closer to him. To be one like we were the night before.

Tuck wrapped his arms around me and pulled me closer. "We're going to have to get up before the rest of the school does. Especially if we're supposed to keep things under wraps like Matteaus asked us to."

I nodded up at him. "Yeah." I sat up and swung my legs over the side of my bed.

Tuck wound his arm around my stomach and pulled me back against him. He pressed his lips to my cheek. "Maybe just another minute."

An involuntary giggle burst through my lips as I leaned back against his chest and let his warm, woodsy scent envelop me. "You don't have to ask me twice."

A loud banging sounded from next door . . . *my door.* We both froze. My dorm room door creaked open, and Ophelia's voice drifted through the wall. "Niche? It's so early. Is everything okay?"

"Not really. We have to meet in the library now. Where's Zinnia?"

We both froze on the spot. I held my breath, waiting for Ophelia to answer. "She's, um, in the bathroom."

Niche growled in frustration. "I don't have time for this. Meet me in the library in fifteen minutes . . . both of you."

"Okay."

The door creaked shut, and I lay there holding my breath.

A moment later, Niche knocked on Tuck's door. We took one look at each other and leapt out of bed. I scrambled around the room, looking for the pieces of my clothing. Tuck froze and stared at me as I bent over to pick up my shirt. When he winked at me, I snatched a pair of his dark jeans from the floor and threw them in his face.

"Tucker Brand! Are you in there?" Niche's voice carried through the thick wooden door.

Tuck cleared his throat. "Yeah, just a minute." He stabbed one of his legs into his pants and quickly zipped the fly. My eyes were drawn toward his flat stomach and the toned muscles that made a perfect V. I bit my bottom lip, and Tuck grabbed my shirt and tossed it in my face. "Focus."

"Right," I whispered.

He pointed to the bed. "Quick. Under it."

"What am I? Five?" I dropped down onto my knees and rolled under the bed, all the while trying not to laugh.

The door creaked open, and Tuck sucked in a deep breath. "Niche?"

I peeked out from under the bed to see Tuck's bare feet blocking Niche's red rubber boots from entering the room. "What took you so long?"

"I just woke up." He sucked in a deep breath. "What's up?"

She shoved into the room, and I pulled myself into a tighter ball and pressed my lips together, trying not to make a peep. "I don't know what happened last night, but you two have a lot to answer for—"

"What happened last night was a magical mishap, nothing more." His voice was so smooth, so calm.

"I'm not sure I believe you. And we will address this further, but for right now I need you and the rest of the crew in the library within fifteen minutes." Her voice was snappy and laced with annoyance.

"Okay, consider me there."

"Oh, and, Tuck?" She paused before leaving.

"Yeah?"

"I'm not happy with our rate of success lately. Things had better change—and very soon." Her rubber boots moved past him out the door.

"I understand." He slowly let the door slide shut behind her.

I waited for a moment before I crawled out from under the bed. I lumbered to my feet and pulled my shirt over my head. "Well, that was . . . tense."

"We're going to have to be a little more careful in the future."

The night before, he didn't look happy about hiding our relationship. Now he was ready to do whatever it took to keep it a secret. Did he regret last night? The things we said? The things we did?

"Hey. I have no regrets about last night." The smile dropped from his face as he strolled over to me. When he turned his warm honey gaze on me, I melted on the spot. He wrapped his hand around the back of my neck and pulled me closer. When his lips met mine, I moved in closer and smashed my body against his. Our tongues wound together, and I dug my fingers into his back, pulling him closer.

He pulled back and glanced down at the bed. "She said we had fifteen minutes, right?"

CHAPTER 10

The moment I walked into the library, I was greeted with complete silence. Every single one of our crew looked exhausted. Tabi slouched back in the chair next to Adrienne. Her eyes were heavy-lidded, and she hadn't even changed out of her pajamas yet. Adrienne rested her head in her hands. Her long braids fell across her face and would've hidden the fact she was sleeping if it wasn't for her deep breathing. Ashryn, our noble elf, sat on top of one of the taller bookshelves with one leg pulled into her side and the other swinging lazily back and forth. When she peered down at me, she saw right through me. Her sharp gaze never missed anything. A slight smirk played on her lips, and she nodded a greeting to me. I quickly returned it. I didn't know what to say at this point or how much anyone else knew. The fewer people who knew about Zinnia and me, the better.

Serrina hunched over with her arms crossed on the table in front of her. Her blond-streaked hair was piled into a messy high bun on her head. Dark circles hung under her emerald eyes. On any other day, she was a carefree goddess-looking witch, but today with her red lips turned into a scowl, she looked ragged and pissed off. "Oh, good. Trouble has arrived."

A moment later, Zinnia walked in behind me and froze at my side. I wanted to reach out and take her hand to show the world we were finally together, and she had my support. But I couldn't. Not yet. Not until I knew what it meant for us.

Serrina rolled her eyes. "And he has company in the form of a power succubus."

Zinnia's eyes darted around the room. "I, um, I'm sorry I lost control. I didn't mean to hurt anyone."

Nova came in behind Zinnia and wrapped her arm around her shoulder. "I was there too."

Ophelia came in and stood on my other side. "That's right. All three of us made a mess of things. At least the hex plaguing Tuck is gone now." She wrapped her hand around Zinnia's elbow and tugged her toward the other end of the table. "Come on. Let's take a seat over here."

"I know I'm not only speaking for myself when I say

there are secrets between all of us and it's not helping. If we're supposed to be a team, then there shouldn't be any secrets." Serrina narrowed her eyes at Zinnia, then at me.

"We handled it." Ophelia glanced around the room. "There was a potion involved, and the magic got a little out of control. I'm sorry if my potion made Zinnia's magic go wild, but would you rather be sitting here tired, or would you rather be mourning the loss of Tuck? Because every single one of you saw him last night, and you know he didn't have much time left."

"Why should we believe anything you say? You're Alataris' daughter." Serrina leaned back in her chair and crossed her arms over her chest.

"Hey!" Zinnia snapped. "We are all standing here alive and well because of her. It doesn't matter who her father is. I would think by now after all she's done to help us you could look past it. But I guess not."

Silence fell over the room, and everyone went motionless, waiting.

Ophelia sighed. "I didn't pick who my father was, Serrina, no more than you chose to be Queen of Desires. I was born into it."

Serrina looked away from them. "All I'm saying is there are secrets here, and we all deserve to know what's going on."

"Every one of us knows exactly what we need to know to defeat Alataris. That's all there is to it." I ground my teeth together. I wanted to tell everyone what was going on, but how could I? Niche made it clear she wasn't happy with what had been happening. I was on thin ice. Would her next move be to send me packing? *I can't go without her.*

Nova made it to the table first and motioned for Ophelia to sit next to her. Ophelia shook her head and moved to sit on the other side of Zinnia. *That's going to take some time to repair.* Like fighting Alataris wouldn't be enough, now my team was divided. In more ways than one.

I wanted to follow behind them and sit next to Zinnia. Instead, I walked farther into the room and sat on the tabletop next to everyone else, waiting for Niche to walk in.

Grayson came in next and silently walked over to me and hopped up onto the table next to me. "You all right?"

After holding Zinnia in my arms all night? "I'm good." I looked him up and down. His button-down shirt was wrinkled, his hair was disheveled, and his skin was paler than usual. "Are you okay?"

"I feel bloody mental. I could barely catch a wink." He rubbed his hand over his face. "Drained is what I am."

I leaned in closer to him and whispered, "Listen, I'm sorry about what happened."

He clapped a hand on my shoulder. "Think nothing of it. We got you both back and healthy. It's part of being a knight. We make whatever sacrifice is necessary to help the queens survive to take down Alataris. I knew what I signed up for."

I thought I knew what I signed up for after the Trials to become a knight. I never could've guessed I'd find my soul mate or end up liking a life I never wanted but always needed.

Beckett walked in next but didn't look as worn as everyone else. His surfer blond hair was damp like he'd already taken a shower. His leather pants and burgundy shirt weren't crumpled in any place, and there were no bags under his eyes. He stopped just inside the door and scanned the room. When he met my eye, he moved to sit on my other side. "You good?"

"I'm good now, thanks to you guys." It was true. Beckett had been there for all of us in a time of need. He kept me calm and sane when Zinnia . . . when she . . . *I can't even think about it.* "You all right?"

He shrugged, and a smile spread across his face. "Never better. I forgot how good it feels to use those powers."

I chuckled. "Your warlock powers are impressive."

"Look, I'm not sure I want to know what happened last night." Niche stormed into the library and slammed the door shut behind her. The bang vibrated the door and made the rest of us fall silent. Zinnia's head snapped up, and she looked around the room with wide sapphire eyes.

Niche stomped over to the table where everyone sat and slammed her hands down on it. Everyone startled and sat back in their chairs. Her flaming hair fell into her face, covering her thick glasses. She leaned forward on her hands. "I get that you're all young, and you have other things on your mind—the Magtrac exams, school, friends . . ." Her eyes darted from Zinnia to me. "Relationships."

I let my face fall into a mask of indifference. If there was one thing I learned through all my training back home in Cindelore, it was how to hide my emotions. I wanted to glance at Zinnia to see if she was thinking the same thing I was, but that'd only add fuel to the fire. Instead, I kept my gaze focused on Niche and nowhere else, even when a few of the others looked at me.

"But now we must put that all aside and do what we were brought together to do." She shoved away from the table and paced back and forth. As she paced, she ran her fingers over the bindings of the books lining the shelves. "I know you're tired. I know you've lost a few matches against Alataris. But we can't lose our edge now." She sucked in a deep breath. "For the past few days, he's been spotted in Central Park making moves. He's readying an army to move on the city."

I barely stayed in my seat. "Are you kidding me? He's going to attack the city, full of humans?"

Niche nodded. "It looks as though he doesn't see us as a threat anymore. For him to be so blasé about his location reeks of either arrogance or a plan to root us out. Either way, he needs to know we are here, and we will continue to contain him for as long as it takes. New York is not up for grabs. I'm not saying we're going to bring down Alataris for good. It would take a lot more than this, but we can certainly do something to stop him from attacking our city."

"But why New York? It's a bold move for sure." The phoenix inside me wanted to move, to fly against him. To hurt him the way he hurt us all. This wasn't just a mission anymore. This was personal.

Niche turned and walked back down the line of bookshelves, running her fingers over the worn bindings again. "I agree. The only reason I can think of that he would try to take over the city now is because if he gets it, he'll have a stronghold in the world. New York is the center of everything. It's ballsy and strong. If he won, who would stand against him? Everyone would be too scared to. So we stop him before he gets what he's looking for."

I tightened my hands into fists at my sides. *Central Park? So close.* Close enough for me to meet him head-on. I had a debt to settle with him. "What's the plan?"

"It's time Alataris faces the full extent of our powers. This isn't like when he attacked us in Hexia. You all have been training for weeks. You've got real life experience now, and all of you are familiar with how your powers work." Niche crossed her arms over her chest. "Rather than sneaking around like we have in the past, I say we get there and surround him and take down as many of his army as we can. And if the opportunity to bring him out presents itself, don't hesitate. Tucker, now that you're back at full strength, you'll take point on this one."

I rose up off the table and stood with my arms crossed over my chest. "Everyone report to the training room in thirty minutes and collect your weapons. We do this . . . together."

Everyone rose from their seats and began to head for the door. Niche moved to stand in front of me. "Are you ready for this? Last time you came face-to-face with him it didn't go so well."

"I'm ready." Alataris had hexed me to try and kill my soul mate, took her mother from her, was trying to rule all of Evermore, reaped the souls of innocent witches and turned them into his mindless servants. He had this and so much more coming to him.

"Very well. I'll see you in the training room."

I gave a single nod. "I'll be there."

Beckett moved to stand by my side. "I'm with you."

Grayson clapped his hand on my shoulder. "What's a little mayhem in the face of a tyrannical ruler? I'm starting to think my uncle isn't so bad . . . wait . . . no . . . I take that back." He shook his head and followed behind them.

"Meet you in the training room." They both left my side and walked out the door. I took a step to follow them, when Zinnia blocked me from going any farther. "We need to talk."

"Something wrong?" I looked her up and down, checking her for any sign of distress. She'd died last night, had been brought back to life, sucked all the powers from the Academy, then gave them back. Not to mention what we'd done for hours after all that. She should've looked exhausted. Instead, she looked happy and refreshed. Even her skin glowed with radiance.

"Not with me." She reached out and pulled Ophelia to her side. "She can't do this just yet, Tuck."

"We need all five queens to do something of this magnitude. You know it, and I know it." When I looked at Ophelia, I almost felt bad for her. She looked more ragged than everyone else. Her long silky hair was a knotted mess down the side of her body, angry red veins forked across her obsidian eyes, and was she wearing two different boots?

"I know, but come on. She just got here, and to send her out to face Alataris so soon? I think we can deal with a blow to his army, but I can't see us taking him down completely without a firm plan in place. This is Alataris we're talking about. Let's go and do some serious damage. We don't need her for it at this point."

I knew Zinnia was Alataris' daughter as well, but she wasn't raised by him like Ophelia was. To Zinnia, he was a stranger, an enemy to be rid of. But to Ophelia, he was *Dad.* I had firsthand experience with what it was like to be raised by a man I didn't agree with. How would I feel if I had to end him? I tried to put myself in her shoes, to think about what it would feel like knowing at some point it was going to be him or me. "Okay, fine. Just this one time. Adrienne was training to take your place. She can stand in for you."

Zinnia wound her arm across Ophelia's shoulders. "See? It'll be okay. And thanks for covering for me this morning with Niche."

"Oh, I bet you heard every word, huh? The walls are

very, very thin." She narrowed her eyes at me. "Keep that in mind next time, Marathon Man, mkay?"

I ducked my head and fought not to laugh outright. "So long as you keep it a secret, I'll be more considerate in the future."

A chuckle burst past Zinnia's lips. "Let's go, O." She steered Ophelia toward the door, and I followed close behind.

Marathon Man.

CHAPTER 11

After all this time, I still struggled to travel through Beckett's portals. My insides turned into a mushy mess, my stomach was in my toes, and my feet were over my head. Strands of my hair blew across my eyes, and I prayed this roller coaster would be over soon. Up ahead, a pinprick of light expanded the closer I came to it. *Ladies and gentlemen, put your seat backs in their upright and locked position. We're coming in for a landing.*

My body tumbled forward and spun out of control. Cool air slammed into my face as I flew through the opening like a bullet. My feet slipped out from under me, and I swung my arms to gain my balance. I face-planted into someone's chest, and two strong hands wrapped around my upper arms and held me back. "Are you okay?"

I looked up into Tuck's warm eyes and righted myself. "Thanks."

"No problem." His fingers lingered on my arms as he steadied me on my feet. Tuck turned toward the rest of the crew. "Fan out in a loose line, and let's start hunting him."

I moved to the center of the group where Nova and Tabi flanked my right side. Serrina and Adrienne took my left. Tuck and the other knights walked beside them. Together, we formed a loose V shape. The sun had begun to set, and a cool fall breeze ruffled my hair and bit at my cheeks. I was grateful I'd chosen my faux fur-lined leather jacket, black jeans, and combat boots. With every step I took farther into the park, my heart raced faster.

I turned down an asphalt path and followed it up over a small hill. There before me stood a light pink glassy dome in the middle of an open field. A small group of boulders rose up along the edges of it. In the distance, large trees stood against a skyline full of buildings extending up toward the clouds. I opened my hand and reached out to touch the dome. "What is this?"

Before I could place my hand on it, Brax wrapped his meaty fingers around my wrist. "No touch." He wrinkled his nose and sniffed at it. "Black magic at work here."

His Russian accent was thick with worry. *How did he get to me so quickly?* Thick black tiger stripes formed on his skin and the pupils in his green feline eyes turned to small slits. One by one, he peeled his fingers off my wrist. Before my eyes, his muscles expanded, and he grew at least six inches bigger. His short crew cut hair lengthened and turned to vivid orange, with strands of gold and black running through it. "Understand, Da?"

I nodded. "I won't touch it." I leaned back and looked up and up and up. "Is this what Niche was talking about? This is his move on New York?"

Beckett moved to stand between Serrina and me. He placed his hand on the dome. Darker sparks of pink electricity forked out from his hand and across the barrier. "It's a cloaking spell."

Nova shifted her weight and sighed. "Then how come the rest of us can see it?"

"It's not meant to be cloaked from other citizens of Evermore. It hides him from the human eye." Beckett motioned to the pedestrians strolling around the park, not sparing a second glance. "Look around. They're oblivious to anything happening here."

"I feel like I want to walk away from it, like it's repelling me." Tabi held both her hands out, and the wind kicked up, sending my hair flying across my face. I huddled deeper into my jacket. Her hazel eyes widened. "The wind goes right through it. Fascinating."

"As fascinating as this is, we need to get in there and see what he's up to and how to stop him." Tuck glanced at Beckett. "You got any magic in your bag of tricks to get past this?"

Beckett rubbed his hands together and eyed the side of the dome. "I think I could come up with something. The question is, what do you want to do after I get us through here?"

Tuck pointed toward a boulder just a few feet inside the dome. The rocky formation was large enough to hide all of us behind it. Hell, we could even spread out in a line on top of it and still never be close to the ground. "We move behind that boulder and see how many troops we are dealing with. Then we choose our battle positions wisely."

We all took a step back and gave Beckett some space. He held his hands out to his sides and expanded his fingers. Blue smoke seeped out of his palms. It crept across the ground like smoke from a fog machine. When it touched the dome, electrical sparks sizzled and forked over the sides like tiny bolts of lightning.

The smell of burnt hair permeated the air, and I wrinkled my nose. "Ugh, it stinks."

"Warlock magic being used against other black

magic can have that effect," Beckett called over his shoulder.

"At some point, we're going to have to talk about this warlock side of you." I crossed my arms over my chest. Was I the only one curious about his past and what it meant for the rest of us? Yes, my father was the king of evil in Evermore, but what was Beckett's story? Was his father close to Alataris? Was he best friends with Dario, Cross' dad? How did this work? Did it bother him to be on opposite sides of his family?

Beckett shrugged. "I have nothing to tell."

More secrets. "I beg to differ."

Before I could argue any more, the side of the dome fractured like a glass pane. Tiny fragments drifted to the ground one by one. It wasn't a shattering. It was a strategic removal of a wall piece by piece. The blue smoke hovered over the jagged edges, making a smooth doorway.

Beckett stepped to the side and waved us through. "After you."

I moved to go through the opening, but Tuck placed his hand on my shoulder and gently pulled me back. "Let me go first, then Grayson. The queens behind him. Brax, Ashryn, and Beckett bring up the rear."

He didn't wait for our response. He turned from the rest of us. White light flashed in the palm of his hand

and his sword slid into his grasp. White hot steel emerged first. Etchings of the phoenix and flames danced across the blade, and he wrapped his hand around the grip. I didn't think I'd ever get used to seeing Tucker summon his sword with his old phoenix shifter magic. He ducked his head and climbed through the opening.

Grayson glanced at me over his shoulder. His fangs shot out of his mouth over his bottom lip. "Steady on, loves. We've got this."

I wanted to rush up behind Tuck and Grayson. It was only a short while ago that Alataris hexed Tuck and nearly drove him to the brink of insanity while trying to kill me. Was it too soon to send him back in the ring for round two? I held my breath and bounced nervously on the balls of my feet. When it was my turn to step through the opening behind Adrienne, I didn't hesitate. The moment I was entirely through the doorway, my senses went into overload. The sounds of clanging swords and orders being barked were deafening. The smell of campfires drifted on the air. I hunched over and jogged to where Tuck and the others hid behind the boulder. Serrina and the others quickly followed behind me.

I pressed my back against the cool rock and glanced

over at Tuck, who was peeking over the edge at the troops. "What do you see?"

He leaned into the group and whispered, "I count at least seventy Thralls lined up, possibly a hundred in formation. And who knows how many more lurking on the grounds. Ten warlocks or so, up front and to the right, are looking over some battle strategies. Alataris is standing up front like a dictator overseeing his troops."

Thralls. I both pitied and hated them. They were Alataris' most heinous creation. He'd taken innocent witches and warlocks who didn't follow him and siphoned all their magic from their bodies. They should've died and been laid to rest. Instead, he used black magic spells to bring them back to life. They were soulless monsters who only followed his bidding. Dangerous didn't even begin to cover what these *things* could do to us or to the humans of New York. The only blessing was that once they were eliminated, they'd turn to ash.

Nova pulled her hair up into a high bun on her head, then tugged her gloves off and slid them into the back pocket of her jeans. She rolled the sleeves of her mesh shirt up and wiggled her fingers, sending sparks of purple magic floating off her fingertips. "What's the plan?"

Brax rolled his shoulders, and a low growl rumbled deep in his chest. "Kill them all."

Tuck swung his sword below his hip. "Yes, but we don't go in guns blazing. There's only ten of us and five times that out there." Tuck glanced over his shoulder across the field.

I turned and stood up on my toes to try and get a clear view. In the center of the field, the Thralls stood still as statues. Their black tracksuits with neon piping told me exactly who they were. Row after row of them stood in military formation, waiting to be commanded to attack. At the head of them all was a small array of tents with a long rectangular table in the center. A group of warlocks cloaked in black stood around maps, pointing and talking. Dario was at the head of the table. I'd recognize that widow's peak and streaming black hair anywhere.

Wonder if Cross knows what his dad is up to.

On the opposite side of the dome, Alataris paced back and forth over a small hill. He was built like a pole with spider-like limbs. His skin was pale and chalky, with beads of sweat running down the sides of his face. A crown I'd never seen him wear before was perched on top of his head. It was gothic looking, with jagged spikes circling his head and a mix of sapphire and ruby jewels just under the spikes in a perfect circle.

So arrogant, the king of nothing!

He was my father, and the only people who knew it were Ophelia and Tuck. I pressed my hand to the cold rock and leaned up on my toes more. "Is he wearing a crown?"

"I think so. I wouldn't put it past Alataris to think he'd need it after he took New York. But that's what we're here to stop." Tuck turned back around to face everyone else. "The queens, including Adrienne, will attack Alataris. Try to take down as many opponents as you can on the way. The rest . . . well, the rest will be up to the knights. You guys have to keep him distracted long enough for us to take out his Thralls and the other warlocks."

I slid away from the rock and looked around at my friends and comrades in arms. "No one gets left behind, okay?" One by one, they nodded. I let my magic flow through my body, and small streams of silver wound down my arms like snakes and gathered in my palms. "Nova, I think we should make it a little sticky for them, don't you?"

Purple sparks flickered on her fingertips, and her lips pulled up in a smile. "I think we can come up with something."

I nodded at Tabi. "Before we go take on the big man, maybe half of his army falls to their final resting place."

The wind kicked up around her, rustling the wild curls that stuck out from her head in all different directions. "I like the way you think."

Flames flared down Tuck's swords. "And my queens." The corner of his mouth tilted up in that cocky grin I hadn't seen in so long. "Let it all loose. Brax, Ashryn, pick them off. Beckett, whatever your inner demons are, let them go. And, Gray, use that speed and rip out some throats. On my count. Three . . ."

My heart thundered in my chest, and I bounced on my feet.

"Two . . ."

Brax let loose a deep growl and threw his body to the ground. He erupted into his tiger form. Black and orange fur covered him. He leapt to his feet and began prowling like he was trapped in a cage.

"One!"

I balled my hands into fists and sprinted over the hill to face an army.

CHAPTER 12

I pumped my arms as hard as I could to make it over the boulder hill. Brax ran by me in his tiger form. With a growl, he dove into the first group of Thralls with his fangs bared and paws lashing out at whatever came at him. Grayson sprinted in circles around Brax, picking off any leftovers.

Tuck ran up beside me. "Don't hesitate."

"Got it."

Wings of fire erupted from between his shoulder blades, and he dove forward, turning into his phoenix form in a flash. I sprinted harder and leapt up in time to land on his back. I stood with my arms out like I was riding a surfboard. Cool wind bit at my cheeks as we soared over them all. I let my powers open up, and I found the warlocks moving toward our crew. I could taste the smoky flavor of their powers on my tongue, see the different colors of their magic shining within them. I shot my magic out like tentacles and latched on to two of them. The last time I faced Alataris, I switched his followers' powers. This time, I drained them both until they passed out cold. Dark magic coursed through my veins, nearly choking me.

I had to get rid of it, get it out of my body now. It burned up my throat, and tears stung my eyes. Last time, I'd given it to another warlock, but none of them deserved these powers, especially if they were going to wield them over the innocent. I held both my hands at my sides, gathering the magic into two identical black orbs. I used the phoenix magic I still had coursing through my veins to light them on fire. "Bombs away!"

I turned my hands to the side and let it drop at the center of the Thrall encampment. They exploded the moment they hit the ground, sending two globes of fire in a twenty-foot radius. Whatever Thrall was near the explosion turned to dust and drifted away on the wind. Across the way, Alataris marched toward the tents and ducked into one.

I pointed down at him. "There, Tuck."

Tuck swooped down low, twisting in close to the tents. He flicked his long tail feathers at the white canvas, and flames shot out of him like a flame thrower, setting the tents into a blaze. Thick black smoke rose up from them, yet I didn't see Alataris anywhere. "Where is he?"

The wind kicked up, and a cyclone scooped up Tabi. Yellow streams of her magic mixed in with it. Its deafening roar sounded like a freight train barreling over everything in its path. A trench of upturned dirt and grass followed in its wake, and Thralls flew off in all different directions. It carried her toward the top of the dome, then suddenly vanished. She plummeted toward the ground. I nearly directed Tuck to catch her when I saw the smile on her face and the determination in her eyes. She held her fist up as she dropped to the ground, gathering her yellow ribbons of magic around it. When she landed in a crouch, she threw her fist down, punching the grassy surface. The ground upheaved as a shock wave expanded in rings out from her. The Thralls stumbled, and warlocks teetered and fell to the ground as they struggled for balance.

Nova walked through the middle of all the chaos as if it were a dance. She dodged Thralls, ducking and spinning in different directions. Purple sparks flew from her fingertips, and skeletal figures rose up from the ground and attacked the Thralls, pinning them to the ground and ripping them to shreds.

I glanced around, looking for Adrienne. We were

going to need her if we faced Alataris. But she was nowhere to be found. "Do you see Adrienne?"

Tuck shook his head and turned to fly another circle over the encampment. Then I spotted Serrina's blond-streaked hair and powdery red magic floating around her. She sauntered up to the warlocks and blew magic across her hand. It surrounded them and drifted across their faces and up their noses. Their body language went from aggressive to passive in an instant. She crooked her fingers at them, and they lined up behind her like a bunch of schoolkids and followed in her wake.

That's when I saw him. Alataris. Running toward the middle of the battle where Nova and Tabi had moved to stand next to each other. "Tuck. There!"

Serrina's eyes lifted to mine, and I pointed to where she needed to be. She held her hand up and made the warlocks stop in their tracks, then she took off running toward the middle of the battlefield. Tucker swooped down low, and I leapt off his back to stand next to Nova. Alataris walked through the mess of his army with his hands clasped behind his back. The sparkling silver crown was tilted at an angle on his head, and he smiled at the three of us standing across from him.

"A valiant effort on your part, really." He gave a bored sigh. "But that's all it is . . . an effort." He held his hands out to the sides like he was the world's greatest showman. "I am the inevitable."

Serrina raced into the clearing and came to a skidding halt next to Tabi. "Dying is inevitable. You, however, are a speed bump on our way to victory."

He shook his head and chuckled. "Ah, the idealism of youth. Take a look around, young queens. There are only four of you, and it'll take all five to harm me. I don't see a fifth around here, do you?"

I glanced at Nova and Tabi. *So, he doesn't know Ophelia's with us. Interesting.*

"It doesn't matter." I summoned my blades to my hands. "Prophecy be damned, as long as we're breathing, we're coming for you."

Tucker flew in low and landed on the other side of Nova, switching from phoenix to man in an instant. White light poured from his hands, and he held his swords at the ready. "I second that."

"Ah, Phoenix. So you survived." A muscle in Alataris' jaw flexed as he ground his teeth together. He looked me up and down with those soulless eyes. "As did you. Interesting."

"Enough." Tabi leapt forward with her sword in hand. She raised it up over her head and brought it down toward Alataris' throat.

From behind his back, he pulled his long dark

sword and held it up, brushing her attack aside as if she were a small child trying to hit an adult. "Adorable."

He shoved his hand straight at her sternum and let it rest there. Tabi dropped her arms. Her sword clattered to the ground, and she arched her back, contorting her body to a painful angle.

Alataris met my eye and snickered. "Something I learned from you, my dear."

He sucked a ball of yellow magic from her chest and held it in the palm of his hand. Tabi dropped to the ground at his feet, lying there lifeless.

I took a step forward. "No!"

"Yes!" He hissed and threw the ball at Nova. It smacked into her like an anvil and sent her flying backward. She lay on the ground, convulsing violently as streams of yellow magic rolled over her. It was too much for her little body to contain both her magic and Tabi's. I didn't know what to do, but I had to do something.

"Alataris!" Tucker's fire wings popped from his back, and he ran at him full force. Their swords slammed together with a fiery hiss. Tuck swung for his head, then his feet.

Alataris leaned back, then leapt over Tuck's blade. "That's right, boy. You've gotten better."

I ran to Nova and siphoned Tabi's magic from her body and threw it right at Tabi.

Nova lay on the ground, sucking in deep panting breaths, and her face was crippled in pain. "That . . . sucked."

Tabi rolled to her side and began to stir. I left Nova and jogged over to Tabi and pulled her to her feet. "You okay?"

She pushed her hair back from her face and nodded. "I think I just died there for a second."

I know the feeling. I motioned for Serrina to come stand next to us. "The only way we're going to win this is if we attack all at once."

Grayson and the other knights continued to battle the Thralls as Tuck fought against Alataris. The four of us rallied around each other. I knew it would take all of the queens we had to do any kind of damage to Alataris. Together we lined up as one, exhausted and beaten down. Yet ready to do battle until we could no longer stand.

Alataris spun away from Tucker and flung a black orb of magic directly at us. I held my hand up and fired my magic straight into it. It ricocheted to the right and smacked into the ground, leaving a divot the size of a basketball. Tucker planted his foot and kicked Alataris square in the chest, sending him flying back.

"Now!" I yelled and hurled myself into the battle. Serrina snapped her wrist out, and her golden whip wrapped around Alataris' neck. She yanked him back, dragging him across the ground.

He wrapped his boney hand around the whip and gave it a tug, pulling Serrina toward him. With one hand, he reached out and sucked her magic from her body. With the other, he fought to loosen the golden rope around his throat. Serrina dropped the rope and fell onto her hands and knees. I threw my magic around the ball like a lasso and shoved it back toward Serrina. She sucked in a deep breath and straightened just in time to take her hit of magic back. She staggered to her feet as I ran past her. I came up behind Alataris and lunged for his neck with my blade. He ducked under it and tripped away from us.

Tucker and I moved as one, stalking toward him.

Alataris held his sword up. "You think you can take me? Well, come on then."

In the distance, Brax's tiger roar sounded. Ashryn's arrows streamed over our heads, holding off any aide who might help Alataris. Nova, Tabi, and Serrina wavered with exhaustion as they came up just behind us.

I glanced at them and back at Alataris. "Oh yeah."

Tucker lunged forward and drew his sword across Alataris' thigh. Blood poured down his pant leg and started soaking the ground. "You can't kill me without the fifth queen."

I shrugged. "Says who?"

With both hands, I swung my blades across my body and smacked them into his sword, knocking it out of his hands. He limped back away from me, and I charged forward, swinging my blades for his throat. One foot away and a short sword came up between Alataris' neck and my circular knife. I jumped back. "What the hell, Ophelia!"

She stood between us with her body turned to the side. "You can't kill him. Not yet."

"Yes, daughter. Yes, that's right." Alataris straightened his stance. "So good to see you . . . *alive*, my dear."

Ophelia's arms shook. Her face was paler than usual and kept shifting from one foot to the other. "Shut up, I'm not doing this for you. I'm doing it for Catherine."

My heart froze in my chest. "My mom. What the hell does this have to do with my mom?"

"If you kill him, she dies too." Ophelia took a step toward me. "They're soul mates, Zin. They completed the pairing. If he dies, she will die too."

"W-what are you saying?" I turned toward Tuck. "Is it true?"

He pressed his mouth into a hard line. "If they

completed the pairing, then yes. If he dies, then your mom will lose her life right along with him."

Alataris pressed his hand to his thigh. Blood seeped through his fingers, yet he didn't seem fazed. He let a devious chuckle loose. "Wasn't quite what you planned." He narrowed his eyes at Ophelia. "It never is. Tell me, how did you survive that fall?"

Ophelia shifted her stance to face him fully, clasping the hilt of her short-curved sword with both hands. "I have my ways, just as you have yours. Five queens, Father. And we are all together. I'd say that puts a wrench in your plans to live forever. Doesn't it?"

His eyes widened as we all stood in a line before him. Each of us was battered, beaten, and exhausted from the events of the night before, yet we stood as one facing the man who wanted to kill us all. The rest of our crew emerged from the chaos of war. Stacks of smoke billowed up from the path of destruction they'd left behind them. The cry of injured warriors and an encampment in complete disarray filled the air.

I gritted my teeth. "Come with us willingly and I promise we won't kill you."

"Won't kill me yet, you mean." He took a small step back. "I think not!"

He threw both of his hands up over his head and hurled a massive energy orb at our group. I threw my magic at it, but it was only enough to make it stop just short of hitting us dead-on. It crashed into the ground before me. My body was thrown back. I tumbled through the air, and my arms flailed wildly. I hit the ground so hard the air was knocked from my chest in a whoosh and my head snapped back. I curled to my side in time to see Alataris running in the opposite direction from us.

The others were thrown back from the explosion. I didn't know where they were or if they were okay. Ophelia was launched off her feet, only to land harder on the ground than I had. She skidded to a halt beside me. A large chunk of skin was missing from her shoulder, and blood coated the ground beneath her. She coughed, and a spray of crimson caked her lips. "At least we shocked him enough to make him run."

I crawled over to her and ripped a piece of the bottom of my shirt off, then held it to her wound. I turned my head up and watched as the camp faded away from sight. *How is that possible?*

"It's a spell, and soon we'll all be left lying in the middle of Central Park exposed." Ophelia threw her arm over her mouth as she coughed. "Where are the others?"

I looked around the field only to see the entire crew lying on the ground riddled with injuries. "My God, they're all down."

"Zinnia, we need to get out of here." Ophelia grabbed my wrist and pressed her fingers into my skin, pinching me.

"You're right." I called out, "Beckett, we need to get out of here before half of New York knows what happened here today."

A few feet away, he sat up with his arm draped across his midsection. "On it."

He placed his hand on the ground, and a portal spilled across it, spreading like a light blue puddle.

I backed away from it. "What the . . .?"

Ophelia dropped through it, disappearing from view. I reached out and tried to grab her hand only to fall into the nothingness of his portal.

CHAPTER 13

TUCKER

I slipped into Beckett's portal before I found Zinnia. I tumbled in his violent abyss. He must've been hurt for it to be this turbulent. My body twisted and turned in all different directions. I was pulled apart and put back together. I tried to right myself, to put my feet forward, but there was no controlling any of it. The screams of my crew echoed in my ears, and I prayed it would be over soon. That one blast, the explosion, had sent all of us flying across the field. I didn't know who was hurt or how badly. A spot of green within the portal rushed toward my face. Before I could brace for impact, I landed face down in the center of the courtyard at Evermore.

Every inch of my body ached and protested as I staggered to my feet. My crew was strewn about the courtyard, each one lying on the ground barely moving. Other students of Evermore rushed out to help us. Some even screamed at our sudden appearance. I spun in a circle, searching for that wild midnight hair, leather jacket and combat boots. My heart was in my throat, and my hands shook uncontrollably until I spotted her kneeling over Ophelia with her hands pressed to her shoulder.

I ran to her side and dropped down beside her. With trembling hands, I reached out and brushed the blood matted hair from the side of her face. "Zin, are you okay?"

She didn't look up at me. "I'm fine."

Crimson rivers of blood ran down her temple and dripped onto her shirt. "You're not okay."

"Tuck, it's just a cut. Look around you. Our crew is down, and they need help." She pressed her hands into Ophelia's shoulder where she held a piece of her shirt over a gaping wound. Ophelia stared blankly up at the sky and sucked in deep, rattling breaths.

"Ophelia!" Cross' voice boomed through the courtyard as he ran headlong toward us.

I moved to kneel on the other side of Ophelia. "What can I do?"

"We have to get her to the infirmary. Now." Zinnia's voice was shaky, and silent tears streamed down her face. "I knew she wasn't ready to face him. Why did she come?"

Cross dropped down beside Zinnia. "I tried to stop her, but she wanted to protect your mother."

"I'm still alive and awake, you know?" Ophelia coughed, and blood sprayed up on my shirt. "You don't have to talk about me like I can't hear you."

"Shit, I think her lung is punctured. We have to move her now." I placed my arms under her legs, about to pick her up and carry her to the infirmary, when Cross brushed my hands aside and lifted her up as if she weighed nothing. Zinnia kept her hand pressed to the wound as they ran toward the stairwell and out of sight.

I turned around to see the rest of our crew slowly moving to their feet. They were bloodied, bruised, and beaten. But we were alive, every single one of us.

Matteaus stormed out toward me. His face was a mask of concern. "Everyone alive?"

I nodded. "As far as I know. Ophelia looks like she took the worst of it."

Niche ran out after him and came to Tabi's side. She threw Tabi's arm over her shoulder and began directing the rest of us toward the stairwell that would take us to the infirmary. "What happened?"

"He had an army waiting and ready to invade New York." Tabi swayed on her feet, and her eyes fluttered shut. When her knees gave out, I moved to her other side and took her other arm. Niche and I practically dragged her up the stairs. Every step we took, her toes caught on the lip of the stairs. Her head lolled to the side and hit my shoulder. Once we made it to the double doors, I kicked them wide-open and lifted Tabi into the nearest bed. As I laid her out, the rest of the crew flooded in through the doors. It'd all been going so well, and then we'd gotten our asses kicked.

Multiple healers hurried to the cots lining the walls. Midday sun streamed in through the oversized windows and reflected off the sterile white walls and floor. Tabi settled on the cot, and her eyes fluttered once more then shut. Her breathing evened out, and every muscle in her body relaxed.

Niche reached out and yanked me to her side. "What happened to her?"

"Alataris siphoned all her powers." I crossed my arms over my chest and watched as Brax refused to be looked at. Grayson rushed from Serrina to Nova and back again, even though blood was dripping from a gash in his thigh. Beckett lay on a cot off to the side, with a healer casting a spell over the side of his face that was swollen beyond recognition.

"My God." Niche turned toward one of the healers. "Her powers, they're . . . they're gone?"

I shook my head. "No, Zinnia saved her, saved us all. She put them back."

Niche sucked in a relieved sigh and asked the healer, "Will she be okay?"

The woman, who was slight in stature and had mousy brown hair and purple robes that swallowed her whole, nodded. "She just needs to rest and reconnect with her powers."

"Thank the Creator." Niche glanced up at me from behind her oversized glasses. "I know you're all injured, but you're alive, and you stopped Alataris from attacking New York. This is a mild victory for us."

I didn't feel like this was a victory. We'd all nearly died. "There's just one thing bothering me. Why would Alataris go after such a big target in the first place, knowing all five queens were still in play? I just don't get it. Why would he expose himself to that kind of potential harm?"

She shrugged. "Who could know the inner workings of a madman?"

"I think I know someone who could." I motioned for her to follow me over to where Ophelia lay on a cot.

The lead healer hunched over her shoulder and held his hands over the wound. His fingers wavered over it like he was playing the piano. Light reflected off his bald head, and his tortoiseshell glasses slid down his nose as he focused his magic on her skin. "Got into another scrape, I see, Mr. Brand."

The air between his fingers and her damaged shoulder shimmered. New skin formed within the wound, and it slowly knitted itself back together. Cold sweat dotted her forehead and matted back into her hair. Zinnia paced back and forth at the foot of her cot, watching the healer's every move. I walked over to stand beside her. I wanted to wrap my arm around her shoulders, to feel her body pressed up against mine, to know she was okay.

I looked at the gash on the side of her head. "You should have someone look at that."

"I can wait my turn. The others are in worse shape than me." She looked me up and down. "Including you."

"What are you talking about?" I felt fine. A few aches and pains, but nothing major.

She faced me fully and reached out. Her cool touch pressed to my bare skin on my torso. Pain ran up my side and down my legs. I hissed in a sharp breath and looked down. My shirt was ripped to tatters, exposing the whole right side of my chest and stomach. *How did I not notice this?* I must've been so worried about everyone else in my adrenaline-fueled haze I didn't feel the pain I did now.

An angry bruise spread over the side of my body, and

I flinched away from her touch. "It can wait. I need to talk to Ophelia first."

"Don't you think you could give her a minute to heal first before you interrogate her?" Zinnia arched her eyebrow and narrowed her eyes at me.

"No, I'll talk to him. It'll take my mind off this." Ophelia blinked down at her mangled skin.

Cross stood up by her head with his arms folded over his chest. "Make him wait, O. You need your strength."

The healer paused for a moment and looked up at the rest of us. "If I may, if the information you need from her is of value, then I suggest you talk to her about it now. Healing fractured ribs in no joke, and I believe one is puncturing her lung. If she doesn't pass out soon, she will at any second."

Ophelia gritted her teeth. "Just ask me already."

"Why would Alataris plan such an open attack on the city knowing we had all five queens together? It seems rather suicidal if you ask me."

When she looked up with those desolate obsidian eyes, I knew I wasn't going to like the answer. She looked away from us all and stared at the wall. "Because he didn't think there were still five queens to face him."

Niche crouched down by her head and ran a damp cloth across her forehead. "What do you mean?"

"She means he tried to kill her and failed." If it were possible for steam to shoot out of Zinnia's ears at that moment, it would. "Right? He tried to kill you, his own daughter. To ensure we would fail in our mission to bring him down."

Ophelia nodded. "He pushed me off a cliff in the Amazon."

"The scream. I heard it before I came up against him when we went looking for the flower to help Tuck. That was you, wasn't it?" Zinnia's cheeks turned an angry pink, and her sapphire eyes flared with power.

"Yeah, that was me." Her face contorted in pain as she gave the healer a dark look. "Ooowwww! Dude, ease up."

"Mending skin isn't the easiest thing, and you've got muscle, tissue, and ligaments to put back together. If I hadn't given you the pain potion before we started this, you'd be feeling a lot more than a few pinches here and there," he snapped and pushed his glasses farther up his nose. "Now, can I continue?"

"Fine." Ophelia rolled her eyes at him, then turned back toward Niche and me. "But I used a spell so I would survive the fall, then I went into hiding to try and figure out how to get here. When I saw Zinnia and Nova at the black market, I knew it was then or never. I made my move." A weary smile spread across her lips. "I'm just glad it worked."

My jaw dropped as I glanced from her at Zinnia and back again. "I'm glad it worked, O. I'm glad you're here."

"Ya know, I kind of believe you." Her brow furrowed, and her body went rigid. I watched as the healer mended the last bit of skin on her shoulder.

"Ophelia, you saved me from making the biggest mistake of my life." Zinnia's eyes glistened with unshed tears. "You saved my mom."

"What is she talking about? You saved Zinnia's mother how?" Niche rubbed at her forehead once more as the healer rose to his feet.

I pressed my hand to my forehead and rubbed at the headache forming over my eyes. "Zinnia's mother and Alataris are a bonded soul mate pairing."

Niche's mouth dropped wide-open, and it took her a few tries to snap it back shut before she could speak. Even then, she only managed one word. "Oh . . ."

The healer held his hands over Ophelia's torso and looked at the rest of us. "If you'll all back away, this part isn't going to be easy." He flicked his wrist, and a white curtain dropped around Ophelia's cot and between the rest of us.

"Wait just a second," Ophelia pleaded. "Cross? Could you just . . ."

Cross didn't hesitate. He ducked behind the curtain and pulled it closed behind him. "I'm here."

Ophelia's ear-splitting screams made everyone else fall silent in the room. Soundless tears streamed down Zinnia's face, and there was nothing I could do for either of them.

CHAPTER 14

Three days later and only half of our crew was out of the infirmary. Miraculously Ophelia left the next day with just her arm in a sling and now stood next to me. I leaned in and motioned to the world around us. "I'm so glad you signed me up for this."

The sun shined down on us and the quiet lapping of waves on the beach calmed the part of me that'd been in a full-on panic since we faced Alataris. This wasn't my first time in this particular room of Evermore, but it was the first time I was technically allowed to be here. Kumi lay in the shallow surf, letting the waves drift over her. Her nine tails swished, sending up little drops of water and sprinkling over the soft white sand. Ophelia adjusted the hand-me-down Ray-Ban sunglasses on her nose. I could see myself in the reflection of her lenses. "I think you needed this."

Nova strolled up beside Ophelia. "We all needed this."

Ophelia offered her a tight smile but didn't respond.

I looked from one to the other. *Awkward.* "Come on, guys. We were getting along before I died for a little while. There's no reason why we can't get along again."

"She threw me into a jail cell using zombies." Ophelia put her hands on her hips.

Nova cocked her hip. "Only after you killed one of my best friends."

"I told you she wasn't permanently dead. I told you to trust me. But did you?" Ophelia shook her head, sending strands of her ebony hair flying around her face.

Nova threw her arms up. "I'm sorry. Haven't you ever made a mistake you regretted? I'm sorry for what I did to you, for losing control like I did." She shifted from one foot to the other.

I needed them to make up. Ophelia was my sister and Nova was one of my closest friends besides Elle. Elle, my childhood friend whom I missed more and more each day. I had to talk to her to ask her how to make amends between these two. She'd know what to do here to make this all better. "Look, guys, I risked my life to save Tuck and both of you were there with me through it. We all made mistakes, but we're still standing here, and I need both of you to get through what comes next. With Alataris and, God, my mom. I don't know what I'm going to do."

Patty Bowerguard, my nemesis at Evermore, as if I didn't have enough already, strolled past us. Her wild curls were piled high on her head and she wore a tiny red bikini. I hadn't even thought to put a bathing suit on for this trip. Yes, we were on a beach, but it was a charmed classroom within the school. I simply pulled my leggings up to my knees and took my leather jacket off and only sported a ripped black tank top. Ophelia wore cut-off shorts and a baggy T-shirt with a faded rainbow unicorn on the front of it. Patty Pinch Face pursed her lips and looked down her slope nose at us. "Trouble in paradise? Or do you all just fail miserably as well, at everything you do?"

Nova started to roll her elbow length gloves off her hands. "Normally I wouldn't be interested in kicking your ass, but today I'm feeling just pissed off enough to take it out on you." She slid her hand out of the glove and purple sparks flared on her fingertips.

"Patty, why don't you go find someone else to annoy?" I turned back toward Nova and Ophelia, hoping to squash whatever this was between them.

"That's right, maybe I'll go find Tuck and see how much he'd like me to *annoy him.*" She practically purred his name and I saw red.

"Tuck has better taste than anything you could offer him." I wanted to rip her hair out. Why did she have it out for me from day one? I'd spent one glorious night with my soul mate, and I felt the connection down to my bones. Yet I was still threatened by this skank. Was it her old family name with ties to the Magical community? Tucker was after all royalty among the phoenix clans. Technically I was a queen, but only because I was the most powerful not because of noble blood.

Patty looked me up and down then wrinkled her nose. "Clearly not."

Kumi spun out of the waves and trotted to my side. Her lips pulled back over her teeth and she growled low in the throat at Patty. *Want me to bite her?*

Yes! Wait, I mean no. No, you can't bite her.

Oh come on, this mofo is asking for it.

I reached my hand out and brushed it through the fur on the top of her head. *Mofo, really? Where'd you get that from?*

Kumi dropped her lips back over her teeth and sat down next to me. *The TV, I think? Brax watches a lot of TV with his pup and his windows are always open.*

I made a mental note to spend more time lounging with Kumi once things calmed down.

"Ugh, put a leash on your mutt, would you." Patty rolled her eyes.

"That'll be enough, Miss Bowerguard." A tall, thin man with swirling chocolate eyes and a hook-shaped nose strolled past Patty straight toward us.

"Professor Howard, I hadn't realized—"

He looked at Patty over his shoulder. "You hadn't realized I was standing right here when you insulted this magnificent creature or when you took it upon yourself to insult your classmate, or even better yet you hadn't realized there is a dress code for all classes here at Evermore?"

Though he towered over me, his shoulders were hunched forward, and he had a soft, kind smile. The sort of smile a grandfather would give his favorite grand-daughter, the kind of smile that reminded me of warm cookies and milk on a sunny afternoon. He held his hand up and snapped his fingers. Patty let out a pained groan. Gone was her little bikini and in its place was a brown sack-like dress that covered her from just under her chin all the way past her knees. She stomped her feet. "Oh noooo."

"Make good choices, Patty." He turned away from her and back toward us.

Kumi tilted her head to the side, studying him. *He smells weird, like a mix of sugar and gravy. Dinner and dessert.* Her tongue lulled out of her mouth and she licked her chops.

You cannot eat my professor. I tightened my grip in her fur just a little.

As if. He's too skinny.

Professor Howard stood unaware of the danger he was in. "What a magnificent creature."

Damn straight I am. Kumi preened.

"Thank you, but she's not mine. More like we belong to each other." I patted her head and stroked just behind her ear.

He leaned his chin down on his fist. "In all my years here, this is the first time she's let me get close enough to her to actually see her true beauty. May I?" He reached a hand out toward Kumi as though he too wanted to stroke her fur.

A low, rumbling growl sounded in Kumi's chest. *He might be skinny, but I'll break something of his, I promise.* Professor Howard froze, not backing down but not moving forward.

Don't be like that. He just wants to pet you. You're a beautiful mythological creature and he's a professor who studies just that. Give him a break.

Kumi huffed and turned her back toward all of us

then sat down once more. Her nine tails swished. *He may not touch the Kumiho. Only on the back of the neck to the middle of my back and no tail. Got it?*

Are we referring to ourselves in the third person now? I snickered to myself as Kumi held her chin up, not dignifying my question with an answer.

"You can pet her on the back of her neck down to the middle of her back." I pointed to the areas Kumi designated. Her midnight fur had an oily look after she rolled in the waves and particles of sand clung to her.

Professor Howard took a step forward and lightly brushed his hand over Kumi. "Fascinating. It feels more like silky human hair than that of a wolf, which has been widely suspected in the magical community. But no one could get close enough to one to know for sure. And she is your familiar?"

I nodded. "We've only known each other a couple weeks, but I couldn't imagine life without her."

Damn straight.

"And you can hear her thoughts in your mind?" Professor Howard took a small step back and hunched farther over her tail. "Do each of these tales have a function? How many incisors does she have? Does she shed seasonally or is it continual? Does her saliva have any kind of power to it?"

The questions were like rapid fire one after another,

and I hesitated. "Um, yes, I can hear her. As for the rest, I'm not entirely sure."

Kumi abruptly stood and began walking away. *I'm done now.*

"What a fantastic creature." A wistful smile played on his lips. "Oh pardon me, ladies. I'm Professor Howard as you may well have guessed."

"Very pleased to meet you. And thank you for allowing us to be in the workshop. I know you only take a limited amount of students." I reached out and shook his hand. Nova and Ophelia followed suit and we all stood in silence for a moment.

Professor Howard gazed out over the ocean and watched Kumi leap and play in the waves. "I might recommend that she move to the other side of the island. The creature we are studying today can be quite temperamental."

Not a chance. I'm staying here. There's no way I'm letting you get eaten or bitten or whatever else he has in mind. I'll keep out of the way.

I let my feet sink down lower into the sand before I looked up at him. "Um, she prefers to stay. She says she'll stay farther away, but she won't leave."

His lips turned up into a smile. "Very well, we'll see if the Peryton minds her presence here."

Oh, that snobby little bitch. He thinks he owns the place, where there are bigger and badder things in this room than him. Namely me!

"She'll be on her best behavior." *Won't you?*

"Excellent, then if you would please move right this way." He motioned for us to gather with the rest of the students who had entered the room. Patty stood off to the side with her two little followers, who were never far behind. Her arms were crossed over her chest and her lips were turned down into a duck-like pout.

Guess she's not used to not getting her way.

I moved to the front of the group. This was a once in a semester experience. The workshop itself usually filled up within seconds of its opening. I was lucky to be here. I glanced at Nova on my right, who had yet to smile, and Ophelia on my left, who still wouldn't make eye contact with Nova. "Come on, guys, we got our asses handed to us a few days ago. The least we can do is enjoy this moment."

"I'm so tired of getting our asses handed to us. There has to be a better way." Nova leaned in and whispered.

The professor cleared his throat. "Now if you'll all look toward the tree line." He held his hands over his head and the air shimmered. An air horn sounded, and I covered my ears. The leaves of the dense foliage rustled. The palm trees swayed apart from each other like the parting of the sea. Then he was here. A glimmer of shining white fur came first. Long, regal antlers popped out next. They spanned at least ten feet and each twisted piece of his antlers ended in a sharp point. He held his nose up in the air and took one step out.

"He's a stag, an albino stag." My jaw dropped. I wished I had my phone in my pocket to take pictures.

"Wait for it, Ms. Heart, wait for it." There was a smile in his voice, and I zeroed my gaze in on the Peryton. When the rest of his body started to emerge, I sucked in a breath. Wings, he had freaking Pegasus wings. They were folded in close to his body. Large white feathers spread over them like angel wings. I wanted to reach out and touch them, to run my fingers through them. The sun glinted off him and he turned to the side and strutted out toward the water.

Such a peacock. Kumi might as well have rolled her eyes at me.

Professor Howard draped his arm across his midsection and bowed. He stayed low, holding that position. The Peryton shifted its course and moved toward us. With his nose high in the air, each lift of his hooves was slow and deliberate.

Professor Howard waved his hand toward the waiting students like a court jester introducing a king to his guests. "Now all of you must hold very still. No one can approach him. If he walks closer to our group, you may reach out and stroke his side. And only his side, understand?"

We nodded in unison and waited as the Peryton moved closer to.

He moved right in front of Nova, Ophelia, and me. I reached out and ran my hand through his white fur. It was thick and wiry, not as smooth as I expected it to be. He shifted closer to us and stood there, not moving.

Patty Pinch Face raised her hand and waved it back and forth. "Professor Howard, Zinnia is hogging all the time with the Peryton."

"It's not as if she controls the Peryton, Patty." He rolled his eyes. "Be patient."

See, he's being such a diva right now. Probably smells me on you. Kumi moved to just out of reach of the surf and was now sitting on the beach, eyeing up the Peryton. She ran her tongue over her canines. *Venison stew sounds good right about now.*

Easy, girl, it's just one class. But the Peryton didn't move.

A smile finally broke out over Nova's face. "He likes you, Zin. I can tell."

"What's it like to be able to read animals so well? Can you hear their thoughts in your mind like I hear Kumi?"

The Peryton leaned his body up against my side and bumped me.

Ugh, you're going to smell now. I just know it. Smell like raw ass. Zinnia the raw ass smelling witch. That's going to be your name from now on. Zinnia queen of smelling like ass. She huffed and slammed down onto her haunches. Sand flew up around her and she sighed.

Don't be jealous, you know you're my favorite.

Nova patted him harder. "No, not so much talking. It's more like I feel their souls. Ya know, queen of death thing."

"That's really cool." Ophelia didn't look at Nova, but a small smirk played on her lips.

On the road to reconciliation? I think so.

I pointed to the top of his head. "He's beautiful. Look at those antlers. They're like his own personal crown." They were sleek and surrounded his head in a halo of glistening white. The Peryton dipped his head down low and gave me a better look at them before he stepped up to the next set of students. "That was awesome."

"Oh my God, that's it," Ophelia snapped.

"I know, right. It's totally his own personal crown." I never took my eyes off the Peryton.

Her hand clamped down on my arm and she yanked me around to face her. "Not him, the crown, Zinnia. That's how we beat my dad. We need his crown."

Nova moved to stand closer to us. "What's Alataris' crown got to do with any of this?"

"Like you guys don't know." She looked from Nova at me and back again. At our blank looks, she chuckled. "Oh my God, you guys really don't know."

For the first time in days, hope bloomed in my chest. I tried to fight it back. "No. Tell us now."

Her lips pulled up it a grin. "The crown amplifies his powers. Well, his power is tied to it actually. It makes him much, much stronger. If we could get it . . ."

My pulse pumped harder in my veins. "Then we could even the playing field." I grabbed onto both of their hands and dug my fingers into their skin. "We need to get that damn crown!"

CHAPTER 15

ZINNIA

I paced back and forth across the blue mats of the training room while wringing my hands together. My combat boots sank into them, leaving an impression with every step I took. The rest of the crew was spread out over the mats in various lounging positions. Silence hung in the air between us. Nova and Ophelia were practically bouncing, but everyone else looked at me like I had twelve heads. Matteaus and Tucker stood behind them all like two towers, both with their arms crossed over their chests and both with lips turned down into equally annoyed scowls.

I stopped my pacing and faced them. "Don't you guys understand what I'm saying? If we take the crown from Alataris, then we might be able to even the playing field.

Lessen his power somehow." Again, no answer. "Someone say something."

"It's dangerous, obviously. But I think you've got the right of it. We need the bloody thing." Grayson leaned back and put his hands behind his head. With his white button-down shirt rolled up to his elbows, the bruises all over his arms from the battle days before were on full display. His normally combed-back hair was a tangled mess, and each time he moved, his face would pull down into a pained frown.

Niche, who was leaning up against the wall, pushed away from it and moved to the front of the room. "This is all well and good, but there are so many problems with that plan."

With one sentence, the wind went right out of my sails. "What? Why is this a bad plan?"

Serrina raised her hand. "Does anyone else not get why this crown is so important?"

Niche tossed her hair over her shoulder and pushed her glasses farther up her nose. "Because it's a piece from the royal class."

"Say what now?" Tabi rolled to her side but didn't sit up.

Niche turned and faced Matteaus fully. She threw her arms up and let them fall to her side. "You want to help me out here?"

Matteaus cleared his throat. "What I am about to say needs to stay within this room. Understood?"

I found myself nodding in agreement along with the rest of the queens and knights. We all sat up a little bit straighter and focused our attention on our headmaster.

Matteaus shifted from one foot to the other and put his hands on his hips. "It's a well-known fact that myself, along with eight other angels, fell from grace. And one of my best friends was the reason we all fell—Lucifer."

My breath stuck in my chest. We all knew Matteaus had fallen from grace, but no one knew why exactly, and it'd been taboo ever since. We're talking millennia of secrets behind the sordid past of the Fallen. I leaned forward, hanging on his every word.

"The moment we arrived on Earth, we were thrown into a war we had no chance of winning. With devil spawn, demons of all shapes and sizes. Lucifer was making them faster than we could kill them."

Oh, my Creator. This was legit history, the kind of history no one knew about. Even Tucker stood next to him unmoving but thoroughly engrossed. "How did you manage? To overcome an enemy who outnumbered you?"

Matteaus pointed toward the ceiling. "The Creator stepped in." He motioned to all of us spread around the room. "He made the world's first supernaturals in an effort to balance the scales."

"The Greeks?" I wanted to bounce on the balls of my feet, but I knew if I did Matteaus might clam up and never continue.

"Indeed, the Greeks." He said *Greeks* like it was a curse. "They were made too powerful for their own good. Even the humans on Earth were aware of their existence, and that wasn't the point of creating them. They were supposed to help us in the Grand War."

Grand War? I'd never heard about any war before. "The Grand War?"

"Never you mind about that. All you need to know is the Greeks were the Creator's first try, and though they were powerful, they proved to be very difficult on so many different levels." His ocean-blue eyes went vacant as if he was thinking of times passed. "Both profession-ally and well, to be honest, personally. I mean, all I can say is do not ever, under any circumstances, date one of them. Let me tell you one time—"

Niche cleared her throat. "Let's not get into those details."

Matteaus walked over to the wall and plucked a knife from the rack. He tossed it end over end and caught it again and again with all the confidence in the world.

"Fair enough. Anyway, after the Greeks, the Creator took it down a notch and made shifters, witches, vampires, warlocks, and anything else you could think of."

"But where does the ruling class come in? I don't get it." Ophelia moved up next to Serrina and plopped down on the mat next to her. She sat with her legs crossed and leaned back on her hands.

Matteaus pursed his lips and kept tossing the knife. "Well, Evermore is ruled in a hierarchy fashion, with the Fallen at the top as the law. The Greeks answer to us like our generals, as much as the Greeks can. I mean, they are real pains in the asses. You wouldn't believe half the shi—"

"TMI," Niche whisper-coughed into her fist.

"Riiigghhtttt." Matteaus sighed. "Anyway, after the Greeks, we have all the other supers. But the populations grew too quickly for us all to maintain. We banded together and felt each species should have a ruling monarch. Those monarchs would enforce the laws of Evermore and report to either the Greeks or the Fallen. Some of you decided to join in the Grand War; others chose to live out their lives among their people."

"But where does the crown come into play? What does it have to do with any of this?" I had to know why it was so important and why it was a bad idea to steal it.

"Because the crowns were made to be given only to the monarchs to amplify their powers so they'd be stronger than any others of their kind. Until Alataris, the system worked beautifully." Matteaus shrugged.

"Are you telling me that Alataris is a true monarch?" *This can't be happening. I'm a princess?*

Matteaus nodded. "He took the crown from his father, the king, and then tied his own power to it. The only way to weaken him is to destroy the crown, to cut off his connection to it so his powers can't be amplified anymore."

"He stole it from his father? What an ass." *Isn't that what you're about to do? Steal it from your father?* I hated comparing myself to him, but sometimes those dark thoughts popped up in my head.

"He killed his father, Zinnia." Matteaus' throat bobbed as he swallowed hard. "He killed him for the throne and the crown."

Was there nothing he wouldn't do for power? "I can't imagine doing everything he's done just to be more powerful. It makes no sense to me at all."

Matteaus gave me a half smile. "Greed will do funny things to you. Trust me. I know."

What did that mean? How did he know? What other secrets was he keeping from us all? "Then why can't we steal it? Destroy it?"

"You can't destroy it because it was forged in heavenly fire and it'll take a weapon of equal fortitude and origins to obliterate it."

Niche moved to stand next to Matteaus. "That's why I didn't go after it. Not only is it dangerous to try and steal it from Alataris, but even if we did there'd be no way to be rid of it once we did. We'd need heavenly fire. More specifically, a weapon to be blessed in heavenly fire."

White light flashed in the palm of Tucker's hand, and his sword was suddenly there. "How about this? It can withstand Phoenix fire, the hottest on Earth."

"That's the point, Tuck. On Earth. You need a blessing from the heavens themselves." Niche ticked off her fingers one by one. "One, you'll need a weapon strong enough to withstand the flames. Two, you'll need a way to get into the heavens, and three, we'll need to make a potion for whoever is going there, so they don't end up dying while they're there."

Ophelia raised her hand. "What do you mean dying?"

Matteaus sighed. "There's a reason why the body expires on Earth and the soul goes to Heaven. Well, if you deserve to. It's because the heavenly plane is made specifically for souls. There is so much power there that the body wouldn't be able to take it. I mean, think about it. That power or magic was used to make all this." He motioned to the world around us. "No mere mortal could take it."

Niche clapped her hands twice, and her clipboard appeared in her grasp. "Not to mention the ingredients for the potion will be impossible to get." She riffled through the pages on her clipboard. "And let's be real, how the hell are we going to find a way up there?" She pointed toward the ceiling.

She's right. Ugh, this is impossible.

Tucker reached out his hand and clapped Matteaus on the shoulder. "Good thing we might have someone who has some ideas about how to get in."

I wanted to laugh. I wanted to cheer him on for his ballsy words. But all I could do was stifle a chuckle. I pressed my hand over my lips and sat still, waiting for Matteaus to say something.

He only gave Tuck a sideways glance. Moments passed until he grunted and nodded. "There might be something I can do. Niche, get all the supplies ready."

The others erupted into cheers, but Matteaus turned his back toward us and looked at Tuck. "You will owe me, Phoenix. I hope you're prepared to pay the price."

Tucker met his gaze and nodded. "I'll pay it with pleasure."

"Very well." Before he could say another word, Matteaus stomped out of the double doors to the training room and disappeared from sight.

I stood and brushed my hands off on my leggings. As casually as I could manage, I strolled up to Tuck. "What was that about?"

"Nothing." He shrugged.

When he looked at me with those sexy honey eyes and a lock of his dark auburn hair fell into his face, I nearly forgot what I wanted to know. I shook his effect off. "Didn't sound like nothing."

"Zin." He sighed. "Let's worry about winning one war before we get involved in another."

I pressed my hand to my head. "I can't even wrap my mind around what you just said."

"Yeah, that about sums up how I'm feeling." He lifted his hand to pluck up a lock of my hair. Halfway there, he hesitated, glanced around at the room full of people, and dropped it back to his side. He leaned in closer to me. "Soon we won't have to hide *us* anymore."

What I wouldn't give just to be with him, to not hide what we were to each other. Sure, everyone might have an idea we liked each other, but not about how much was between me and my soul mate. "I love you," I whispered.

"I love you, too." His warm, woodsy scent enveloped

me, and flashes of the night we'd spent together ran through my mind. I was so close to him. A few more inches and I could brush my lips against his.

"Zinnia!" Niche's voice snapped across the gym.

I jumped back and away from Tuck. "Um, yes?"

She crooked her finger at me. "Come over here."

Ophelia and Nova were already standing at her side when I got there. Was she going to call me out in front of everyone for lusting after my secret boyfriend? *Boyfriend?* Sounded so minor for what he was to me.

I tucked a lock of my hair behind my ear. "What's up?"

"I need supplies for the potion I'm going to have to make for whoever goes up to the heavenly plane." Niche riffled through some pages on her clipboard.

I looked from Niche at my friends and back again. "Who do you think will go to the heavenly plane?"

"I'm not sure. But you can't expect them to let heavenly fire be brought down to Earth, silly. The only problem is if a living being goes up there . . . well, they might explode from the power. So a potion is what we'll need." She bit at her bottom lip. "A very powerful one at that."

"Okay, what do you need me to get?"

"Angel feathers." She beamed up at me and then moved on to talk to Tabi and Serrina.

"Angel feathers. Right, no big deal. I just gotta go pluck an angel. I'm sure they'll like that." *How the hell was I going to get angel feathers?*

Ophelia wagged her eyebrows at me. "Guys, I think I have a plan."

CHAPTER 16

OPHELIA

An hour later, we were all in position. Though the courtyard was surrounded by the school on all four sides, there were plenty of hallways for Matteaus to escape down and even more classrooms for him to duck into. I pressed my back to the cool stone wall. Students passed by me, each one giving me sideways glances. A girl who was a year ahead of me stopped dead in her tracks and stared at me. Her wild red curls were pinned high on her head, and she wore a green plaid skirt and bright yellow sweater. Her lips turned up into a sneer. In all the years I'd been locked away with my father, I never let anyone push me around. And I wasn't about to start now.

I waved my hand like I was flicking away a fly. "Move it along, peon."

Her jaw dropped, and she held her pointy nose in the air. "I can't believe you're a queen. What a waste of power."

I crooked my finger at her. "Why don't you come a little closer and see how much power I can waste?"

She clutched her books closer to her chest. "Like I'd give *you* the time of day."

I shoved away from the wall and dusted off my hands. "Well, you know what they say."

"No. What's that?"

"There's no rest for the wicked." I stretched my hands over my head and yawned. "That's probably why I'm always exhausted."

I took a single step in her direction, and the girl shrank away from me. She scurried away with a squeak. A light chuckle escaped my lips as I leaned back into position to watch Matteaus.

"Toying with the commoners, I see." Cross' smooth deep voice ran over me like ice on a hot summer day. I was calm and nervous at the same time. Something about him was so alluring yet so forbidden.

"Cross." I looked up into his gold eyes and fought the urge to beam at him, though my heart did little flip-flops every time he came close to me. I didn't smile at him. I didn't even flinch. I'd learned to hide my emotions long ago, and I certainly wasn't going to show them to Cross Malback of all people. The guy had a slew of female warlocks and witches parading in and out of his room at all hours of the day and night. I refused to be one among many. *No, thank you.*

"Careful, O. If you start to look happy to see me, I might think there's something wrong with you." He pushed his hair out of his face only to have it fall right back into his eyes. *Ugh,* why *does he have to be so hoooottttt?*

"I'm not happy to see you." *Liar, liar pants on fire.*

His lips pulled up into a half cocky grin, and he turned his body to lean up against the wall next to me. When his shoulder brushed mine, a current ran between us and goose bumps broke out over my skin.

He leaned in closer to my ear, and his breath tickled my neck. "Keep telling yourself that."

"Why bother, when I'll forget we had this convo a second after you leave?" Again, I lied. Tonight, I might lie in bed listening to Zinnia sleep and think about every nuance of this conversation.

He shook his head and tsked at me, then lifted his hand and ran his finger from my shoulder down to my wrist. "How long until I wear you down? You and I both know there is no one else in this world who understands you the way I do." His lips brushed over my ear. "Who will challenge you the way I will? I'll challenge you in ways you can't imagine."

Am I on fire? I feel like I might be on fire. "You and I both have things we need to accomplish. Why add more to the drama when I will only be the flavor of the week to you?"

He pushed away from the wall and turned to face me full-on. He was so close. His ocean scent hung in the air between us. It reminded me of the wildness of the sea, and of the wildness in him. When he put his hand on the wall behind me and leaned in, I thought he might kiss me. I was excited and terrified at the same time.

"Flavor of the week?" He shook his head. "Ophelia, it would take a lifetime to savor you."

Smooth. So smooth. "Play on, player." I turned my back to him before my treacherous body gave anything away.

"Come on, O. What's it going to take for you to believe me?" He moved around me and caught my eye. He held his arms out. "I'm here. In *Evermore Academy* because of you. A place we both know I don't belong. I've put all my plans on hold to be here. The least you could do is give us a chance."

Two more students, a boy and girl, stopped on the other side of the hallway and began whispering to each other. Both had beautiful blond hair and bright blue eyes and looked like they stepped out of a magazine. No doubt they traveled back to Malibu for every break in their convertibles to soak up the sun and make their skin even tanner. They peeked over at me, then the whispering started all over.

I stomped my foot. "Ugh, what?"

They jumped, but the boy was the first to speak. "Aren't you Ophelia?"

"Yeah, so?" I shrugged.

"I-I wanted to k-know . . ." he stammered.

They always wanted to know something. Did your father really try to kill you? Are you evil? How could you be a queen? Why are you so pale? Who's your mother?

I held my finger up, silencing him. "Let me stop you right there. Yes, my father did try to kill me. Yes, I am the Queen of Potions and Spells. No, I'm not evil, and yes, this is starting to annoy me. Does that about cover it?"

The boy shook his head. "T-That's not why I'm here." He looked at the girl next to him, and she shoved him in the shoulder for encouragement.

I glanced over Cross' shoulder to see where Matteaus stood, still talking to a student as he pointed to the fountain, while the younger student made frantic notes in his spiral-bound notebook. I could tell from the way Matteaus patted the boy on the shoulder I only had a few more minutes, maybe seconds, to accomplish what we needed to. Across the way, Zinnia was making the slash mark across her neck and pointing at the people around me. *Yeah, I'd like them all to stop talking too, sis.*

I turned back toward the boy. "Okay, spit out whatever insult you got and be on your way. I have things to do, junior."

"Can you please tutor me in potions?" He screamed so loud that the other students around us stopped to stare.

My jaw dropped, and I looked from Cross, who couldn't contain his laughter, back at the kid. I was shocked, stunned, flabbergasted, and speechless. Whatever the hell it was when someone was beside themselves, I was it. He tugged at the straps on his backpack and held his breath, all the while rocking back and forth from his heels to his toes. "I'm failing. And if anyone could teach me, it has to be a queen, right?"

In theory. I sucked in a breath and blew it back out. "Are you serious? You're not screwing with me?"

He glanced over his shoulder at the girl. In that moment, I saw the resemblance. This had to be his sister. She nodded at him, and he looked back at me. "No. I really do need help."

"Um, yeah, okay, kid, I'll help you out. But we have to start next week. I'm kind of in the middle of something."

A wide grin spread across his face, and if possible, his

cheeks turned bright red. His eyes glowed with excitement. "Thursday. Can we start on Thursday?"

"Um, sure." I looked at Cross. "What day is today?"

He pressed his hand over his mouth and held his laughter in. "It's Thursday."

I clapped my hands together. "Great, so yeah, next Thursday evening. I don't do mornings, kid. Six o'clock in the potions lab?"

"Yes! Okay. I'll be there." He leapt back and grabbed his sister's hand. "Come on, Chelsea, come on. I told you she wouldn't kill me on the spot." He tugged his sister so hard she tripped after him as they ran down the hall.

Excited because I'm going to tutor . . . what just happened?

"Did that just happen?" I leaned back on the wall. "Did a kid actually ask me for help?"

Cross nodded. "Tell me about it. I've been asking you for a date for months now and I get nothing. The pipsqueak asks you for tutoring and *boom*! He's got a study date with you in the library."

I gave his shoulder a light push. "He's not trying to make me another notch on his belt. You are."

He rolled his eyes. "I'm not. You're important. Just tell me how to prove it to you."

A small patch of the stone block lifted up at my feet, and a skeleton hand popped out. I jumped back. "What the hell?" The thing snapped its fingers at me and pointed toward the courtyard. I turned and glanced up to find Nova waving her arms at me then pointing to Matteaus. "Gotta go."

Cross wound his fingers around my upper arm and held me in place. "First tell me how."

"Fine." I pulled my arm free from his grip. "My father tried to kill me, and I plan on returning the favor. And I know you have plans for your father and family. Once our respective tasks are complete, then we can give"—I motioned between the two of us—"whatever this is a try."

"You're saying once we do what we both came here to do is done, you'll go on a date with me?"

I shrugged. "Essentially yes." *What am I doing? A date with Cross Malback?* Other girls had lost a lot of things to Cross on just one date. The kind of things you couldn't get back.

The skeleton hand sank back into the ground, and I was left alone with him once more. *I'm going to have to talk to Nova about that freaky shit.*

Cross' tongue darted over his bottom lip. "Deal."

My heart jumped into overdrive. "Great, so I gotta go." I leaned against the corner and peeked around it, watching as Matteaus began to stomp down the opposite hallway.

"Just a second." He grabbed my arms and spun me

around. His lips crashed over mine, catching my surprised gasp. They were soft, full . . . *delicious.*

His spicy cinnamon flavor invaded my mouth. I melted against him. His body was so much bigger than mine. When he wrapped his arms around my lower back, I felt like the two of us were fused together. My body went wild, and I was sure this time I was on fire. My hands wound in his shirt of their own accord, and I pulled him closer. I wanted more. I wanted this all the time. An endless amount of this!

Crap, crap, crap. It took everything I had in me to shove him away. With both hands, I pushed his chest as hard as I could. He stumbled back only a step. His lips were swollen and damp from my kiss. He brushed his thumb across his bottom one. "Oh, O, that was so sweet."

My hand shot out and snapped across his cheek. The sound echoed in the hall, and people stopped to stare at us once more. I arched my eyebrow at him. "You deserved that."

He rubbed at the angry handprint on his cheek. "Maybe, but it was worth it."

When he took a step toward me, looking as if he was going to grab me again, I held one finger up. "Stop right there." He froze.

I had two choices. I could run away and let him have

this win. Or I could leave with a victory and the upper hand. *Upper hand it is.* I pushed him back up against the wall and wrapped my hands in his shirt. I held my lips a breath away from his and rubbed the tip of my nose against his. "You don't get this." I pressed my body up against him and slowly lifted a hand to his mouth. I ran my finger lightly over his lips. "Until we *both* get a victory."

Cross leaned forward, about to kiss me. I backed away, not giving him what he wanted. He cleared his throat. "Ophelia, you just assured me I'd win."

"So confident in your skills?" I turned away and started walking toward Zinnia and Nova waiting for me by the fountain.

"No," he called after me. "Beating him was important before."

I froze and looked at him over my shoulder. "And now?"

"Now it's essential." He straightened his stance and squared his shoulders.

"Well, just remember I don't share with others, so until then I suggest you keep your lips and hands to yourself. Otherwise, the deal is off." *There's no way he'll let me stop him from seeing other girls. Watch him buckle in three . . . two . . .*

"As long as you're taking as many cold showers as I am, I'm in."

I schooled my features, not showing the surprise I felt. "Well then, game on, Cross."

"Game on."

"Ophelia! Let's go!" Zinnia called out to me. I turned away and ran because if I looked at him any longer, I might toss away the whole deal and go back to kissing those delicious lips of his.

CHAPTER 17

ZINNIA

Nova clapped her hands together. "Woohoo." She placed two fingers in her mouth and whistled.

Ophelia lifted up both of her hands and flipped off Nova while running out to meet us. "Shut up."

"That was some kiss." I wanted to hug her the way a sister might, throw my arm around her shoulder and pull her in close to find out exactly what just happened between her and Cross. Instead, I held off, not knowing what exactly to do. It seemed like so long ago when I made the deal for her to stay in Evermore Academy in exchange for her silence about our family connections. The more time I spent with Ophelia, the more I felt I needed to tell everyone she was my sister. *Another secret to take care of.*

"Ugh, both of you shut up." She waved me toward the hallway Matteaus just disappeared into. "Let's go."

I grabbed her arm, stopping her. "Are you sure we shouldn't just ask him?"

"Right because he's going to let us pluck him like a chicken." Sarcasm dripped from her every word. "Would you come on already? I promise this will work."

The three of us tiptoed after him. I pressed my hand over my mouth to suppress my laughter. I hadn't done anything like this since I was a kid.

Ophelia pointed at a black feather on the ground. "Look, there's one."

I bent down and quickly scooped it up. "Do you think one will be enough?"

The feather had an oily sheen to it, and when I ran my fingers over it, it felt like nothing I'd ever touched before. It was the softest cotton, the smoothest silk, and lighter than air. "I expected this to be like a raven feather. But just feel this."

I held the feather out toward them.

Nova brushed her fingers over it, and her eyes went wide. "Wow, we definitely need more."

Ophelia pressed her hand to it. "Even if we don't need more for the potion, we definitely need more. I think I could make a dress out of this."

"I think he went that way." I pointed down the hall

and around the corner. "Let's see if we can find some extras." This was one of the first missions I went on that wasn't life or death, the first time I felt like a teenager on a scavenger hunt. *Next up, steal a pair of Tuck's underwear.*

A breeze drifted down the hall, and another black feather tumbled over the stone floor toward us. Nova dove to the ground and snatched it up. "Mine."

Ophelia grabbed my hand and tugged me forward. "Come on. I want one too."

We were jogging around other students and laughing the way we might've done had we grown up together as real sisters. When I glanced at Ophelia, her face went from beaming like a little kid to wide-eyed. Before I could look forward, I slammed into a brick wall. Wait. No, not a wall. Someone's torso. My face mushed into his ribcage, and the air whooshed from my lungs. I ricocheted off of him like a pinball and fell onto my ass. The palms of my hands scraped against the ground as I caught myself.

I lifted up on one butt cheek and rubbed it with my hand. "That's gonna leave a mark."

"What in the hell are you three doing? Making a down comforter?" Matteaus put his hands on his hips and looked down his nose at me.

Ophelia hauled me up to my feet. "We were just collecting feathers." She gave him a palms-up shrug.

"For what purpose, exactly?" The muscle in his jaw ticked as he ground his teeth. "I'm not some goose you can just pluck for your own amusement."

Nova ran up beside me with two more feathers in her hands. "It wasn't for a blanket."

I leaned in and whispered, "Not helping."

"Well, someone better start talking, and they better start talking fast." Power rolled off of him in waves. I felt it with each passing moment. As a Queen Siphon Witch, I was more attuned to it than most. To me, it was like sunbathing. I had more energy, and I felt alive.

"Niche said that in order for us to go up to the heavenly plane to get a weapon blessed by heavenly fire we'd need a potion so we wouldn't die up there. Like our bodies wouldn't be able to contain our spirits or something. So, we need angel feathers as an ingredient for it." I held up the feather in my hand and waved it back and forth to emphasize my point.

Matteaus closed his eyes and rubbed at this forehead. "Creator, help. These kids are going to be the death of me, I swear." He sighed. "You need an angel feather . . . not a fallen angel feather. I'm fallen. I've been stripped of heavenly powers. The best these feathers will do for you is stuff a pillow."

"Oh." I didn't drop mine on the ground. I wanted to keep it. It was beautiful and a token of the first time O and I had some fun together. Sure, it was short-lived, but I appreciated it anyway. "Any idea where we could get an angel feather from an angel who's not fallen yet?"

Matteaus threw his hands up in the air. "I suppose I could think of something." He shifted from one foot to the other and let go of a heavy sigh. "Yeah, okay. I'll think of something."

"Thank you. We owe you big time." I held his black feathers tight in my hand.

Matteaus turned from me, mumbling, "You can't interfere, only guide them. Ten seconds in the room with the prick and I'd have this whole mess straightened out. But no, now I gotta trap a freaking angel . . ." He continued his muttered tirade until he was entirely out of sight.

"That was intense." Nova pulled her backpack around to her front and tucked her feathers inside.

I nodded. "Yeah, it really was."

"Guys, did he just say something about trapping an angel?" An evil grin came over Ophelia's face. "Badass."

I am going to get in so much trouble for this!

CHAPTER 18

TUCKER

"I don't understand why I can't just fly there." I shuffled from one foot to the other. Dawn was upon us, and cold dew clung to the grass in the courtyard. Early morning fog settled across the ground, and I could see puffs of smoke with every breath I took. Nervous flames kept springing up in the palms of my hands, and I squeezed my fists, extinguishing them before anyone else could see.

Zinnia motioned to Grayson, Serrina, and herself. "One, because none of us can fly. And two, because you don't even know where we're going."

"I think this is something Gray and I can handle on our own. There's no need to endanger both of you." In truth, Zinnia had died in front of me only a few days earlier, and I wasn't ready to live through something like that again.

"Bugger off, mate. Niche said we take the queens, then we will bloody well be taking them. I get it you're good with your fireworks and I'm fast as hell—and well, the better looking of the two of us—but we need their magic." He gave me a playful punch in the arm.

I rubbed at the spot where he hit me. "I just wish Beckett were well enough to come along. A portal would be great right about now."

Serrina tossed her hair over her shoulder. "Have you looked at his face? The healers are doing their best, but that much damage is going to take some time to mend. Another hit and he won't be so pretty anymore."

Zinnia narrowed her eyes at me. "Can I talk to you for a second?"

"Niche said our ride would be here at any second." From the way she was looking at me, I wasn't sure if I wanted to have a private conversation with her. She only narrowed her eyes, crossed her arms, and ground her teeth together when she was annoyed at me.

"Now." She walked past me and grabbed my jacket, dragging me to the far corner of the courtyard, where we were out of earshot but close enough to jog over the second our ride got here.

She released my jacket and rounded on me. "What's your problem?"

"I don't have a problem," I lied.

"Liar. Either you tell me what's going on in that head of yours, or I'll go to Niche and tell her something is wrong with you, and Nova can come with us and you can stay here and babysit Brax's puppy with Kumi by your side."

God, I love her. She was so fierce, a force to be reckoned with. She pulled her wild hair into a high ponytail. I looked at the ground and kicked at a rock at my feet and whispered, "You died." I held my hands out in front of me. "I held you in my hands. Your lifeless body was just here."

Visions of her cold dead body assailed me. I never wanted to see her with her eyes closed and not breathing again. The knife in my chest twisted, and I lost my breath. It was too fresh in my mind. I needed her. If I was going to live in this world, I had to do it with Zinnia by my side or not at all.

She ducked her head to meet my eye. When I finally looked at her, she sighed. "Oh, Tuck, you think I don't know what it feels like? I watched you go insane for days, and finally, when I thought I'd lost you completely, Ophelia came up with a solution of how to help us. This is who we are. This is what we were born to do."

I nodded. "I know that. I really do. But, Zin." I swallowed around the ball in my throat. "I can't watch you put your life on the line every day."

"Well then, maybe Niche was right." She threw her hands up and let them fall to her sides with a slap.

"What are you talking about?" I wanted to reach out and pull her into my arms, to hold her there and keep her safe.

She stepped in closer to me, and her warm sugary vanilla scent surrounded me. I knew I couldn't live a day without it. Then she jabbed her finger into my chest. "The reason why couples are forbidden in our group is because of this exact situation. We have a job to do, a destiny to fulfill here." She lowered her voice. "He's my father, Tuck. And I was born to stop him. What does that say about all this?"

Zinnia was right. I knew she was. "I'm just struggling."

"I get it, I really do. But not letting me go on missions that are this important to the crew is not helping. If anything, you'll get us all killed sooner." Large shadows passed over us, and Zinnia glanced up at the sky then back at me. "You need to decide now. Either you're all in, or you need to stay behind and let me do what I need to do. Because I love you, Tuck. I really do. And I can wait until this is all over to be with you if that's what you need. But nothing, and I mean nothing, will stop me from trying to take down my father. Not even you."

She was right. We had jobs to do. Lives we were born into. I couldn't look past her death, but I could look forward to the rest of our lives. And if they were going to be long lives, then I had to get my shit together, for her, for myself, and for Evermore. "Zinnia, I don't want to wait to be with you. But you're right. We have to face this."

Her lips pulled up into the smallest smirk. "We are better together than we are apart anyway. Besides that, who else's room am I going to sneak into at night? I mean, you do have the best pillows."

"You love me for my pillows? Really?" I chuckled.

She looked me up and down. "And other things."

"Oy, you lot. It's time." Grayson pointed toward the sky. Four large creatures circled above us like vultures waiting to pick at our dead carcasses.

"Time to go." Zinnia motioned toward where Grayson and Serrina stood. "Are you in or out, Phoenix?"

"With you? I'm always all in." I wanted to take her hand, to walk with her toward our destiny. But I didn't. Instead, I walked as close to her as I possibly could and stayed with her every step of the way.

CHAPTER 19

The sun glinted off large brassy metal wings as they came closer. I shielded my eyes from the glare. "Are those metallic Pegasus?" *No freaking way!*

Tucker nodded. "Matteaus said we'd need a weapon strong enough to withstand heavenly fire. There's only one person on Earth we can get one of those from: Hephaestus."

Seriously? I couldn't believe it. "Like the Greek god of metalwork? The one who they say got thrown off the side of a cliff by Hera, his mother?"

Tuck leaned in so close to me I could feel his breath tickle my ear. "And you thought you had a bad parent?"

I stifled a giggle. "True enough."

They drifted down closer and closer to us. Their wings flapped and moved as elegantly as any swan I'd seen, though they looked like something out of a steam-punk magazine, with exposed bolts, brass finishes, and metal joints. As they glided toward the ground and put their feet out, I expected for them to take a few steps to slow down. Instead, they planted their feet and skidded to a halt, leaving deep trenches in the grass behind them. They lined up like soldiers, one right after another. Their eyes glowed a bright green like the *on* switch of a coffee machine.

One of the metal Pegasus in the middle stepped forward. A small door opened in the center of its chest, and a single envelope popped out.

Tuck waved his hand forward. "Go on. Take it."

I moved toward the machine slowly, taking calm steps one at a time like I was approaching a live stallion. The metal Pegasus didn't move. I pinched the envelope between my fingers and pulled it from the door. Once I removed it, the door slid back into place. I tore into it and held up the thick parchment for us all to read.

Dear Witch Court,

It is with my esteemed pleasure that I receive you at my forge. The favor you ask is no favor at all. I will be happy to provide you with a weapon of your choosing to suit the purpose for which you seek. My Pegasus are equipped with the coordinates of my most treasured secret. Should this secret be revealed to any others, you will all suffer.

Grayson made a sound of disgust in the back of his throat. "He's got a screw loose?"

"Shut up, Gray. What other choice do we have?" I waved the paper at them as I continued to read it.

As I promised Matteaus, you will all arrive alive and intact. Rest assured my Pegasus will keep you safe until your arrival. I look forward to meeting you, young warriors. - Hephaestus

"Did anyone else see the part that said *until your arrival?*" Serrina walked over to one of the Pegasus at the end of their formation. She placed her foot in the stirrup and hiked herself up, throwing her other leg over the back of the Pegasus like a true cowgirl.

"I noticed that." As I approached the one at the center, steam shot out of its nostrils. I hesitated.

Tuck leapt up off the ground and landed with two feet on the back of the Pegasus next to mine. "Are you okay?"

I shrugged to hide my nervousness. "So long as I'm not riding anywhere with Hermes, I'm good."

"When did you fly with Hermes?" Tuck dropped down into a seated position on the back of his machine and grabbed the reins.

Grayson ran to stand beside me, and a chuckle rumbled in his chest. "When she kicked him in the face and off a magical platform."

Tuck did a double take when he looked at me. "You did what?"

"Well, he tried to kill me first." I shoved my combat boot into the stirrup and held on to the saddle. I hopped on my one foot and hoisted myself up. With a not-so-ladylike grunt and definitely not as graceful as Serrina, I swung my leg over the saddle.

I tilted to the side, about to slide off the opposite side. Tuck reached out one hand and steadied me. He whispered, "I can't believe you did that. That's my girl."

I beamed and centered myself on the back of the Pegasus. The metal was cool under my legs, and a chill ran over my skin, sending goose bumps all over my skin. I wrapped my hands in the leather straps and squeezed my legs together. "Okay, I think I'm ready."

Before anyone said another word, the Pegasus took off, shooting straight up into the air like a rocket. My stomach dropped into my feet. I wrapped my arms around the neck of the machine and held on for dear life. Wind whipped past me, and my blood froze in my body. Shivers racked me from head to toe. All my life I pictured what it would be like to ride on a Pegasus through the clouds, gliding along so gracefully like a swan or crane. They were graceful, smooth and beautiful. At this second, I had a rocket in the shape of a horse between my legs.

My hair blew in all different directions, and my fingers froze in their clutching position. We moved so fast that my stomach had yet to catch up. But once it did, I was sure I was going to regret it. Behind me, Grayson whooped and hollered. Of course, the speedy vampire was enjoying the ride. Tears fell from my eyes, not from crying, but from the cold wind smacking me in the face. It bit at my cheeks and went right through my black leather leggings.

"Zinnia, you okay?" Tucker called out to me.

"F-finneeee." I was not fine. "J-just c-c-cold." My teeth chattered so hard I thought I might crack one in half. When I glanced at Serrina, she wasn't faring much better. She too was huddled on the back of her machine, shaking from the cold air at this height.

"You are not fine. Hold on."

I tried to peel myself up from the horse, but I couldn't. Then it dipped down, and a warm weight settled behind my back. Tuck's arms came around me, and I was flooded with his phoenix heat. The muscles in my body slowly unclenched, and I leaned back into his chest. My teeth still chattered. "W-what a-about Sssss-errina?"

"I've got her covered." I hadn't noticed how close he steered us toward her ride. We were side by side. Only a few feet away.

She sat up straight and squared her shoulders. "Thanks, Tuck. You're like the best kind of space heater."

He moved his head to my other side, where no one could hear him. "Would you rather I ride with her?"

I let go and dug my hands into his thighs. "No."

"Jealousy is a good color on you."

He was right. I was jealous. Serrina was gorgeous, the Queen of Desires. Any girl would be envious of her. But Tuck hadn't given me a reason to be jealous, nor had Serrina.

I cleared my throat. "I trust you, you know?"

"I know." He squeezed his thighs in closer to mine and wound his arms tighter across my stomach. My heart thundered in my chest. Would there ever be a moment when my pulse didn't race? When I didn't get butterflies? Or when I just wanted to be around him to hear what he thought or felt?

Too soon we were diving down toward a small island off the coast of a large peninsula. "Where are we?" I looked out over the aquamarine water, the white sandy shoreline and the multicolored terracotta homes embedded in the side of the mountain. I'd only seen pictures like this in travel magazines. "Oh . . . my . . . God . . . are we in Greece?"

Tuck pointed to the island that was steadily getting

bigger as we came closer. "Yes, but it looks like we're landing on one of the smaller islands off the coast."

I sat up straighter on the horse and leaned forward for a better view. The smell of the sea surrounded me, and I felt a sudden sense of ease. Like because I was closer to the ocean, everything was going to be okay. The Pegasus dipped lower, and we glided down, heading toward the side of a mountain at full speed. My frantic pulse raced in my veins. Just when I thought we were going to crash into it, two double doors that I didn't know were there swung outward. I cringed back into Tuck's chest. The trees in front of the doors folded into the ground, and from within the cave, bright lights flashed like a runway at an airport. My body lifted out of my seat, and Tuck held me down harder.

My heart was in my throat. I was going to puke and pee all at the same time. There was no way that door was big enough for all of us to fit through. The machine tilted to the side, and we slid through with less than an inch of space between my leg and the metal doors. We entered into what looked like an indoor soccer field, minus the goals, lines on the field, and teammates. The ground approached so fast I didn't have time to brace for the impact.

"Gray, get Serrina!" Tuck bellowed.

"On it!" Grayson stood on the back of his Pegasus in

a crouch. Then shoved off with his legs, launching himself at Serrina. His chest smacked on the back end of the horse and he clung to the saddle. He pulled himself up by his fingertips then wrapped his arms around Serrina, tucking her in close to his body. "Get ready for a rough landing!"

The Pegasus landed the same way they did in the courtyard of Evermore Academy. They jabbed their feet down into the ground and abruptly stopped. My body flew forward right off the horse. I soared through the air like I'd been thrown from an ejector seat. Tuck wrapped his arms around me and pulled me into his chest. The heat around me intensified, and gusts of warm wind drifted across my face. In my peripheral vision, I spotted the edge of his flaming wings. He slowly came to a stop. Grayson raced by with Serrina tucked carefully in his arms. He too slowed his pace until he could stop.

Tuck placed me on my feet and sank down into the bright green turf.

I grabbed onto his shoulder to steady myself. "I think"—I swallowed hard—"I might puke."

CHAPTER 20

Zinnia pressed her hand to her mouth and shook her head. "No, nope. I think I'm good." She sucked in a breath through her nose, then puckered her lips and blew it out. She bent over at her waist and put her hands on her knees as she continued to suck in those breaths.

Serrina stumbled up beside Zinnia and plopped down on her butt. She sat cross-legged with her hands out behind her. Her face was a sickly green color, and a sheen of sweat covered her face. "Holy hell, that was awful."

Grayson shot me a sideways look, and his shoulders wiggled with the laughter he held in. I turned my back to the queens and stifled my smirk. Grayson and I were used to moving at fast speeds, but they hadn't been exposed to it on a regular basis.

"Are you two laughing?" Zinnia's voice was laced with disbelief.

We both spun back around at the same time, and I pressed the back of my hand to my lips. "No, it's just . . . please don't puke or pass out." I glanced at Grayson. "Maybe this is something we're going to have to work on in the future."

Zinnia stood up straight and put her hands on her hips. "It's not like we're training for NASA. You don't have to put me in one of those spin thingies just to get me ready for G-force speed."

"Well, don't look at it that way, love. Look at it as more of an anti-puke prevention training." Grayson clapped me on the shoulder.

This time, I couldn't hide my smile. "It's something we'll have to look into."

A screeching growl sounded around us, and my blood froze in my body. The familiar sound of a snarling feline predator sent chills down my spine. Zinnia's eyes widened as she focused on a point beyond my shoulder. I slowly turned around to come face-to-face with a herd of oversized mechanical manticores, and I was suddenly back in the trials—the event that brought me here to

Zinnia, to being one of the knights to protect her. Flashes of Niche's lifeless body surrounded by these creatures ran through my mind. It was my job to protect her, and now I would do the same for Serrina and Zinnia.

Grayson shoved his hand inside his jacket and pulled his throwing stars out from his inner pocket.

I glanced down at them. "What are those going to do to a manticore?"

"Check the necks, mate. The metal is softer there. We might be able to cut through."

The huge metal lions had bat-like wings and the tail of a scorpion. Hephaestus made them from an aged silver metal. Their eyes glowed a fiery red, their teeth were sharpened into razor points, and they circled around us. The sound of clanking metal and gears grinding filled the room. Grayson moved to stand in front of Serrina. He bent his knees and narrowed his eyes on the encroaching herd. When I moved to stand in front of Zinnia, she reached her hand out and touched my back. I felt the slightest pull on my powers, then it subsided. It wasn't enough to fatigue me in any way, but it was enough for her to be loaded with ammunition.

She stepped out beside me and held her hands up. Flames lit the palms of her hands along with her silvery magic. "Bet you're happy you brought us with you now."

"You bet your ass." In one hand I held my sword; in

the other a ball of fire. There were only four of us against a herd of at least ten mechanical manticores.

Serrina shoved Grayson to the side and held her long golden whip in her hand. She flicked her wrist back and forth, making the whip crack and move like the tail of a snake. "I'm ready."

One of the lions lunged toward Zinnia with its razor-sharp paw held high in the air. He swiped down toward her face. Zinnia twisted away as I swiped my sword upward, knocking the lion's paw aside. Zinnia threw her hand out, tossing the fireball right into its chest. It sounded like the striking of a gong when it struck into the lion. The beast flew back and smacked into the rocky wall. It dropped onto the ground, and part of the wall crumbled over it, pinning it to the turf floor.

Serrina swung her whip out. It cracked as it wrapped around one of the manticore's neck. The machine extended its wings and pumped them. It launched straight up into the air. Serrina was yanked off her feet. Her head snapped back, and an ear-splitting scream ripped from her throat. I forced my wings from between my shoulder blades. Light from the flames illuminated the area. With one pump I was airborne, shooting up toward the sky after Serrina.

The manticore twisted and turned in all different

directions, taking Serrina with him. I held my arms out. "Serrina, let go. I'll catch you."

She held on a moment longer until the manticore took a hard twist and dive bombed toward the floor. Serrina was shaken loose and tossed to the side like a rag doll. Her arms flailed in different directions. I pulled my wings in tight to my body and pushed them out hard, pumping them furiously. The rocky wall quickly approached. I dove forward and shoved my body between Serrina and the wall. She smacked into my chest, knocking the wind from my lungs. My back cracked against the jagged rocky surface, sending dust flying over us. We ricocheted out toward the middle of the cave, hovering in midair. I twisted in uncontrollable circles, grappling to stop us from spinning. Serrina slipped from my grasp, and I swung my arm out and caught her by her fingertips.

"Don't let go of me!" She bucked her legs and reached up toward me with her other hand.

My hands were slick with sweat and adrenaline flooded my body. Every passing second, she slipped a little more. "I won't drop you." *Please, God. Don't let me drop her.* We were at least a hundred feet up with only the hard ground below us.

On the other side of the warehouse-like cave, Zinnia and Grayson stood back to back, fighting off the encroaching manticores. They prowled closer to them only a few feet away. I held my wings out, letting the flames flare and drift us down toward the ground. One of the beasts prowled just below Serrina. It chomped its teeth at her dangling feet. I held her up, trying to keep her fingers from sliding any more.

"What in the devil is going on in here!?" A deep, loud voice boomed, and then everything went to utter crap.

In unison, the manticores all turned to look at the giant man. He stomped into the middle of the field and jabbed his fingers at them. "Bad kitties!" His deep baritone voice boomed, and the manticores cowered away from him. Their eyes switched from glowing red to green.

The one under Serrina flopped over on its back, exposing its belly to us. I slowly pulled my wings in and drifted toward the ground, letting Serrina touch down first.

I landed beside her. "Are you okay?"

Her streaked blond hair was a tangled mess, her white V-neck T-shirt was ripped across her midsection, and her jeans had dirty smudges all over them. She leaned over and sucked in a couple deep breaths, then dusted her hands off on her pants. "Yeah, I think I'm okay."

Zinnia jogged to Serrina's side. "My God, are you okay?"

"Aside from my hand hurting a little, I'm fine." Serrina bent and flexed her fingers, then cracked her wrists.

"Right, sorry about that. They get a bit protective. That's the way I designed them." The man stood at least eight feet tall and had long bright red hair that ran down past his shoulders. The wild curls twisted and tangled around each other. A thick beard the same color as his hair covered his face and ran down to his belly button. He had a bulbous nose and full red cheeks. A jagged scar ran across his forehead, through his eyebrow, and down the side of his face. Part of his eyelid drooped down from where the scar had knitted back together. The skin rose up and was stark white against the rosiness of the rest of his face.

The manticore nearest to Zinnia moved in closer to her. She froze. To anyone else, they might think she was terrified, but I knew differently. Magic swirled down her arms and into her hands. Then the beast curled its head under and rubbed its body up against her side the way a house cat might—a house cat that was a thousand-pound machine.

Zinnia cringed as she reached her hand down and

patted the manticore on its smooth metallic head. "Um, good kitty?"

I extended my hand out to the giant man. "You must be Hephaestus."

"Indeed I am." He took my hand—and by hand, I meant he took my whole lower arm, including my hand, and shook it. My shoulder nearly popped out of the socket, and my toes lifted up off the ground when he moved his hand up and down.

The moment he let go, I had to roll my shoulder to make sure it was still in place. I swung my arm across my body and rubbed my bicep with my other hand. "Pleased to meet you."

He hiked up his canvas pants, then hooked his thumbs into the top of his belt. "And who might you be?"

"Matteaus sent us for the weapon." Grayson swatted away one of the manticores that tried to rub up against him.

Hephaestus crossed one hand over his rotund belly, then with the other he rested his chin on his fist. He gazed up toward the roof like he was seeing other universes within his silvery eyes. "Never heard of him."

We all exchanged sideways glances. Serrina looked at me and mouthed the words *what the hell.*

Zinnia pulled the envelope he'd sent to us with his Pegasus from the pocket of her leather jacket and handed it to him. "Perhaps this will help . . . jog your memory."

Hephaestus snatched the envelope from her hand and tore it open. He held it close to his face, then farther away, then close again. He squinted his eyes. "Well, so I did. So I did." He shoved the letter into the pocket of his pants. "I'll have it with you in just a couple hours."

"Um, you do know we need a weapon strong enough to withstand being blessed by heavenly fire, right?" I didn't know why I felt the need to clarify. Maybe it was the confusion on his face, or the fact he didn't remember sending the letter or his Pegasus for us.

"Right, of course." He tapped the side of his head. "I remember."

Sure you do. The two heavy doors we flew into slammed shut with a resounding bang. I swallowed down my uneasy feeling. "How long do you think it'll take?"

Hephaestus threw his hands up and shrugged. "An hour or two." He motioned to the cave-like warehouse. "Make yourselves at home. Explore the island if you like. We'll meet back here at dinner time. It's been a long time since I've had *guests.*" He stared at us for a long moment, then backed out the door.

We all turned to face each other in a huddle. Serrina

was the first to speak, "Yeah, that wasn't creepy or concerning at all."

I nodded. "I have to admit, I'm worried."

"What is it with the Greeks? Are they all"—Zinnia held her hand to the side of her head and twirled her finger around in a circle—"ya know, crazy?"

"They're a sorry lot, I tell you that. Completely daft, mental even." Grayson poked me with his elbow. "What's the plan?"

Zinnia nodded. "We definitely need a plan. I don't trust any of them."

My mind raced. They were right. Hephaestus seemed out of sorts, just like the rest of the Greeks. They were extreme everything—extremely powerful, extremely emotional, extremely eccentric, and extremely dangerous. But we needed them. We needed *him*. "We need the weapon. He's the only one who can forge one strong enough to withstand the fire. Without the weapon, there will be no destroying the crown."

Zinnia nodded. "So we get that first, and then we get out of here ASAP."

"Exactly. Grayson and Serrina, you guys check out that half of the island." I pointed in the direction Hephaestus went. "Zinnia and I will go in the opposite direction. Remember we need to find a way out and a way to actually get back to Evermore."

"Right, come on then, love." Grayson threw his arm over Serrina's shoulders and guided her toward the other end of the warehouse toward the door Hephaestus went through. A team of manticores followed in their wake.

"Do you think we're in trouble?" Zinnia looked up at me with those deep sapphire eyes, and I couldn't lie to her, not even to reassure her for a second.

"I'm not sure. But my gut is telling me we are." My inner fire burned hotter. The wings at my back wanted to pop out to protect her. We were alone and surrounded by oversized house cats.

I stepped in closer to her, ran my hand down her arm, and took her hand in mine. Her warm vanilla scent enveloped me, and I wanted to drag her up against my body. Every time I looked at her, she twisted up my insides and made me hope for the future. Hope, something I hadn't let myself have until I met her.

Now standing here worried about our lives, I only knew two things. We were going to get out of here because I had to know what a future with her would be like. And I loved her more than my own life.

Shit. We need to get out of here.

CHAPTER 21

Outside Hephaestus' stronghold, I walked alongside Tucker, climbing over rocks and around bushes. The steep incline of the inactive volcano gave my legs and back a workout so intense sweat ran down the sides of my face. I'd long since thrown my leather jacket over my shoulder and was now standing in my loose-fitting tank top that hung down a little too low in the front and sides. My hair was in a knot on top of my head.

Tucker pressed his hand to my backside. "Careful you don't trip."

I glanced at him over my shoulder. "Did you just make up an excuse to grab my ass?"

"Can't fault a guy for trying." He snickered and

stepped up beside me and pressed a kiss to my temple. "Besides, you've been swinging it in my face this whole time. What'd you expect me to do?"

My heart fluttered in my chest, and I leaned into him and wrapped my arm around his waist. Our bodies fit like two puzzle pieces coming together. In the distance, the sound of trickling water caught my attention. "Do you hear that?"

Tuck tilted his head to the side, listening. "I think I do. Come on." He stepped out of my arm and took my hand, tugging me through a thick patch of bushes.

I sucked in a deep breath. "Wow."

There before us was a hot spring the size of a small pool. Steam rose up from crystal-clear water. I bent down and stuck my hand in. It was warm to the touch.

"Come on." I rose to my feet and kicked off my combat boots.

Tuck arched an eyebrow at me. "What are you doing?"

"Look at me." I held my hands out to my sides. "We're stuck on this island until the weapon is ready, and I'm filthy. A little dip won't hurt anyone." I hooked my thumbs into the waistline of my pants, and with one yank I pulled them down past my knees and shimmied out of them. Tuck stood with his mouth gaping open as he stared. I kicked my pants at him. "Are you coming in or just watching?"

He ran his tongue over his lips. "I'm having a hard time deciding. Are you wearing a bathing suit?"

I glanced down at my black bra and matching panties. They stood out against my pale skin. "Nope."

In one swift movement, he pulled his T-shirt over his head. It was my turn to stare at the corded muscles covering his body. His tan skin glistened in the sun, and for a moment I forgot we were on a mission, forgot the weight of the world rested on our shoulders, forgot my secret sister and horrible father. I was a normal teenager on an island with my soul mate, the guy I was destined to be with for the rest of my life.

He froze with his hand on the button of his fly. "Now who's staring?"

"I can't help it." I motioned to his abs and beautiful face. "How could I not look when you've got all of that going on?"

Tucker unbuttoned his pants, then drew the zipper down. All I could hear was the sound of my own breathing. When he dropped his pants and stepped out of them, I ran my eyes over him—from his dark auburn hair, past his black boxer briefs, to his perfectly toned legs. He was stunning . . . and all mine.

He stepped out of his pants, strutted past me, and dropped down into the hot spring up to his hips. When he smiled at me over his shoulder, I nearly melted in the hot sun. "This was your idea. Aren't you coming in?"

My pulse raced in my veins. I wanted to jump into the water, to wrap my arms around him and never let go. Instead, I stumbled forward and tripped into the water. Water splashed over him as I found my footing. When I stood up straight, it came up just above my belly button. It wasn't quite as warm as a hot tub, but it was comfortable and refreshing, and I felt the sweat washing away. I let my fingers hover over the surface. I caught Tuck watching my every move. I squirmed under his gaze. "It's so warm."

"It's from the volcano. I suppose Hephaestus keeps the forge going with it even though it's supposed to be dormant." He stepped in closer to me. "Come here."

He opened his arms for me, and I stepped in closer to his chest. We sank down lower into the water. Tuck cupped his hands around the back of my thighs and lifted me up. I wrapped my legs around his hips as he moved to sit on a small rock shelf in the pool. Tuck brushed his hand down the side of my face and caught a strand of my hair between his fingers. "When this is all over, I want us to have a normal life. Go on dates—normal dates like dinner and a movie, not steal a moment alone when we're on a mission." His brows furrowed, and his lips turned down.

"Hey, if it wasn't for this life, I wouldn't have met you." I pressed a kiss to the ridge between his eyebrows. "One day we will have our date." I kissed the corner of his mouth. It turned up into a smile. "But for now, let's be grateful for what we've got."

He rubbed his cheek against mine, then met my eyes. Heat pooled low in my belly and I wanted more of him. I'd always want more. "Until then." He pressed kisses up and down my neck. "I'll steal every moment I can with you."

I love you. I love you. I love you.

"I love you, too," he whispered against my skin.

Shit. Did I say that out loud?

His mouth was hot against my skin as he left a trail of kisses down my neck and across my shoulder. His hands slid up my sides and across my back to the clasp of my bra. With one sly movement, I felt it give way and slide down my arms. I tossed it aside and wrapped my arms around his neck, pulling him closer. I pressed my body against his. His warmth felt amazing against me, and I wanted more of him. Closer. I needed him so much closer. I dug my fingers into his skin and held him to me.

Clank, clank, clank. Metal upon clanking metal sounded.

We both froze. I glanced over my shoulder and threw my body against his for a whole other reason. "What the hell?"

"Pardon me." The robot's mechanical voice was halted and stiff. He looked like a golden version of a butler, complete with a golden tux, combed-back hair and a fake smile in place. "Your presence is requested in the dining hall immediately. Should you choose not to attend, you will be forcibly brought back to the main house."

Tuck wrapped his arms around my back and held me close, shielding me from the robot as much as possible. "We are coming," he growled.

The robot didn't move. It just kept staring at us with those fake metal eyes, like he was once a human man but was dipped into bronze.

Tuck flicked his wrist and splashed him with water. "Turn around."

The robot stiffly moved to give us its back. With each step it took, it clanked and grinded, crushing the grass beneath its feet.

I shoved my hand down past the surface of the water and snatched up my bra, then quickly threw my arms into it and snapped it on within seconds. "We couldn't even get a minute."

"I'd like to think I take longer than a minute, thank you very much." He chuckled as he climbed out of the pool and offered me his hand.

I giggled and took his hand. "That is so not what I meant." I looked down at my soaking body. "This is going to be fun trying to get my clothes back on while soaking wet."

Steam rose off Tuck's body, and in an instant he was dry. "I don't know what you're talking about."

I held my arms out to my sides. "Okay, do me."

Tuck coughed into his fist. "That's what I was trying to do before he showed up."

"Oh, you have jokes now?" I raised my eyebrow at him.

He stepped into his pants and pulled them up and quickly fastened them. "Just a couple." He held his hand out in front of himself, and a blast of heat came at me. It was like standing in the baking sun in the middle of a dessert. The hot air wafted across my body like a blow-dryer.

Every drop evaporated from my skin, and my under-wear dried in record time. "Thanks."

He bent over and tossed me my clothing. "We better get moving."

I gave the hot spring one last longing glance and sighed. "Okay."

THE WAREHOUSE FIELD had been transformed into a large dining hall, complete with a U-shaped table with all the chairs facing the center of the room where we all now stood. Grayson and Serrina were covered in sweat and grime. I almost felt guilty for having the chance to rinse off . . . almost. At the center of the table, Hephaestus sat with a goblet the size of a bucket and a golden plate stacked high with an abundance of food. At least two turkey legs stuck out from the pile of mashed potatoes and stacks of grapes and apples.

He threw his hands up into the air. "Ah, my friends. Welcome, welcome." He waved us forward. "Please join us."

The rest of the seats at the U-shaped table were all taken by robots identical to the one who retrieved us from the hot spring. A chill ran up my spine, and goose bumps broke out over my skin. Eerie silence hung in the room between us.

Tuck stepped forward and gave a slight bow. "With respect, Hephaestus, we're expected back at Evermore

Academy. So if you could please kindly give us what we came here for, we will be out of your hair."

His words were so smooth and confident, yet I felt uneasy standing there with only four of us against a whole army of machines. Hephaestus glanced around the room at the empty plates in front of his machine men and then at us. He held his plate up. "There's plenty more. My other guests don't eat much."

He slammed his hand down on the table and let out a loud barking laughter. His barrel chest rumbled, and he tipped back in his chair, laughing at his own lame joke. The robots all laughed in unison, a monotone *ha . . . ha . . . ha*. That left me feeling cold.

At the same time, they all went silent.

Tuck didn't waver. "Regrettably, we must be going."

Hephaestus unfastened a belt around his waist and threw it onto the table in front of him. It landed with a thunk. On Hephaestus, the sheath on the belt looked like it held a dagger. To any of us, it would be a small sword made for quick, precise movements. The silver hilt glinted at the end. In the center of it where it was to be held, a thick leather strap was wound tightly around it. Onyx jewels sparkled within each of the three points in the cross shape of the sword hilt. My eyes locked onto it. That was the sword that would hold the heavenly fire, the sword that'd destroy Alataris' crown and put us on a level playing field. This might be the first time in history the queens came close to taking him down. After centuries of his reign and his continual extinction of the queens who came before me, I finally felt a spark of hope. We might be able to stop him and save Evermore from the war he was trying to start.

Hephaestus motioned to the sword. "You get that after you eat. You've only been here a few days. You might as well have a meal before you go."

I sucked in a shocked breath. "A few days? We've only been here a couple hours."

He tapped his pointer finger to his chin. "Did I forget to mention time moves differently on my island?" He threw his hands up. "Oh well. What's a few more hours or hell, a few weeks? I am enjoying your company, as I'm sure you're enjoying mine."

Grayson stepped up next to Tuck and lowered his voice. "Say the word and I will snatch it and we run."

Tucker held his finger up to Hephaestus. "A moment, if you please." He turned to Grayson and whispered, "Run to where?"

"Serrina and I found a mode of transportation if you found a way out." He looked around at the robots. "I don't think they're going to let us be going."

"We need that sword." I ground my teeth together. "I am not leaving here without the damn thing."

Serrina crossed her arms over her chest. "None of us are."

"Well?" Hephaestus rose to his feet and put his hands on his hips. "Shall I ready your rooms? A vacation will do you some good."

"A vacation? More like imprisonment," I muttered.

Like a set of dominos, the mechanical butlers rose to their feet one by one. We were surrounded on three sides.

Tuck glanced around and pressed his lips together. "Unfortunately, we don't have weeks or months to spare. We will, however, come back to visit if you'll just let us leave with the sword. I give you my word."

Hephaestus' face turned down into a scowl, and he waved a dismissive hand toward us. "Not good enough. It's been years since I've had visitors." He narrowed his eyes at Tuck. "You will stay, and you will enjoy my company."

The robots all marched out from behind the table. The clanking of their stomping feet was deafening. They chanted, "You will stay. You will stay."

"Time to go, mate." Grayson held his arms in a runner's stance.

Tuck nodded, and adrenaline flooded my body. We were going to fight our way out. It was now or never. Who knew what kind of contraptions he had to hold us prisoners? I wasn't going to wait around and find out.

Tuck whispered to us, "Three . . . two . . . one!"

Grayson raced forward. He was a blur moving through the room. He skidded to a halt at the center of the table, gave a salute to Hephaestus, and snatched up the short sword. He jetted back to Tuck's side. "Let's move."

I turned toward the only exit available and prayed it would lead out. Grayson was in front of us, Serrina was by my side, and Tuck was bringing up the rear.

"After them, now!" Hephaestus' voice boomed.

We ran headlong into a tube-like hallway. My breaths came in puffs as I pumped my arms, running as fast as I could. Behind me, a wave of heat exploded in the hall. I glanced over my shoulder to find Tuck lighting everything on fire.

He pointed ahead of us. "Go. Keep moving!"

Up ahead, I spotted the end of the hall that looked like it opened up into a barn. Grayson skidded to a halt in the middle of all the stalls. "We were here before." He pulled a small box from his pocket with wires and antennas hanging out of it. "We've got a ride."

Tucker stood at the opening and blasted stream after stream of flames into the hall, holding off the butler boys. "Whatever you guys are going to do, do it now. We haven't got much longer." Sweat ran down his face and dripped onto the floor. His T-shirt was soaked to his body.

Serrina opened a stall in the back corner of the barn and walked in. When she came back out, she led a team of four mechanical Pegasus all hooked up to a gleaming golden chariot with wings and horses etched into it. Their eyes glowed a warm green, and they pranced with excitement the same way a pack of real horses might. The bridles were connected and ready to go.

Grayson jumped into the chariot and took up the reins. "Hop on."

I shook my head. "I'm not getting on that thing. It's controlled by Hephaestus. We'll be killed."

Serrina forced open a set of doors, and the sun shined in so bright I had to shield my eyes. "We took the remote antenna off of it. We should be able to control it now."

"Should be?" I hesitated at the back of the chariot.

Tucker ran up behind me. "We have no other choice." He bumped me forward and I stepped up onto it.

Serrina jogged back behind the chariot and loaded up behind him. Tuck turned and grabbed her to move her in front of him.

"Right. We all sorted?" Grayson cracked the reins, and the chariot shot forward.

My body jerked, and I bumped into Tuck's muscular chest. He pressed his hand to my back. "I've got you."

The mechanical butlers flooded in just as we took off. When I looked back, I spotted Hephaestus standing at the edge of the barn with his fist raised. He was screaming something I couldn't make out. We were moving away too quickly.

I sucked in a deep breath. *We might be okay . . .*

CHAPTER 22

ZINNIA

"This is not okay! What the hell are we going to do?" I clung to the edge of the chariot and hunched down behind the edge. The sky was pitch-black. In the distance, the four towers of Evermore Academy called to me. They were surrounded by the bright lights of New York City. If we could only get there, we'd be okay. The four Pegasus were fighting against each other. A moment ago, half of our team's eyes had switched from red to green once more. Hephaestus was gaining control over them. The chariot whipped around, and my legs went airborne. I held on to the side for dear life.

The school was quickly approaching as we came crashing down. The chariot jumped up and down. The entire thing rattled as the horses rammed each other with their bodies. I wanted to close my eyes, to not watch what was about to happen. But we were like a train wreck about to happen. I couldn't look away. I froze with fear, helpless to do anything but hold on.

Tuck wrapped one of his arms around my waist and his other around Serrina. "I've got you."

The chariot shot straight up into the air, then fell sideways. Blood dripped from the reins wrapped around Grayson's hands, yet he didn't let go. He looked at Tuck. "Save them!"

"Wait, no!" I reached out to grab hold of him, but my fingers slipped off his shoulder as Tuck opened his fire wings and caught the wind. We drifted behind the chariot as it twisted straight up into the air like a tornado. I shoved at Tuck's chest. "No, we have to save him."

"Stop fighting this! I have a plan." He jostled me in his arms. "Do you trust me?"

I nodded, never taking my eyes off the careening chariot.

Tuck pulled his wings in, and we plummeted toward the ground in a freefall. My stomach crashed into my toes. The wind whipped past my face, and the school became clearer as we fell. At the last second, Tuck opened his wings about ten feet from the ground and dropped Serrina and me into the courtyard. I hit the ground hard, so hard my bones rattled and my legs buckled. I rolled to the side and flopped onto my back.

High above us, I watched as Grayson fought to keep hold of the chariot and Tuck pumped his fire wings furiously toward it. Flames trailed out behind him. The chariot went completely vertical and paused for a moment in midair before it fell straight down. Tuck tried to turn out of its way but ended up getting thrown back inside of it with Grayson.

I flung my hand over my mouth. "No!"

Matteaus marched out into the middle of the court-yard. "What's happening?"

I pointed up to the sky. Tears pricked the back of my eyes. "They're crashing."

The Pegasus all had glowing red eyes now, and they were headed straight down into the center of the court-yard. Matteaus stepped out in front of the fountain and held his hands out. Tabi and Nova ran to my side.

Ophelia marched out to me and grabbed my hand. "What's happening?"

"They're coming down!" Serrina screamed.

Yellow streams of magic shot from Tabi's hands and into the ground. Vines flew up behind the fountain, weaving together into a vast net. The first two Pegasus crashed right in front of Matteaus. The ground shook, and it sounded like an explosion. Tuck wrapped his arms around Gray as they both were ejected out of the chariot. Matteaus held his ground in front of the crashing chariot. He reached out, trying to catch them, but they flew through his grip. Tuck forced his wings out, but it was too late. They smacked into Tabi's net. The vines gave just enough to cushion them, before they were thrown back out and onto the ground.

They rolled to a stop and were barely moving. Matteaus turned and slammed his fist into the second set of Pegasus that crashed into the ground, and the chariot hit him head-on. It sounded like a bus colliding with a train. Metal screeched and groaned as it contorted around his bulky body. Matteaus and the chariot hit the fountain at the same time. It shattered into a burst of dust and rocks. Water sprayed up like a geyser. Tuck and Grayson staggered to their feet, and we all stood gaping open-mouthed at the destruction. The courtyard was completely destroyed. Mounds of dirt were everywhere, jagged contorted metal was spread over the ground and Matteaus was buried somewhere under the chariot, along with the fountain. Doors up and down the hallways flung open, and students poured out to see the scene around them.

Everyone was clad in their pajamas, watching in shocked awe. The five of us stood side by side, with me at the center of all the queens. I stared at the pile of rubble on top of Matteaus. Low whispers of if he was dead or not spread through the crowd. I took a step toward the wreckage and rolled my sleeves up. "Well, don't just stand there. Help me dig him out."

I reached out to pick up a rock when the whole pile started to shake and move. I stumbled back. Matteaus' hand shot up from the ground, and then the pile exploded outwards, sending dust and rubble flying. Matteaus flew up from the pile like a rocket. His black wings reminded me of raven feathers. They were strong and shining. It was the first time I'd ever seen him fly. I was in awe of how beautiful his wings were, so strong. I felt pulled toward them, like the magic alone could draw me in.

He flapped his wings and slowly came to a graceful landing right next to the pile. He kicked a rock back onto the fountain pile. "Why?" He pointed his finger toward the heavens. "Kane! Is this your idea of a joke?"

Ophelia looped her arm through my elbow. "Who is he talking to?"

"I have no idea."

"Damn fountain. Why is it always the fountain?" Matteaus kicked another rock across the ground. Feathers fell from his wings as he stomped back and forth, pacing like crazy. He spun in a circle, then bellowed, "Bed! Everyone back to bed!"

Tuck moved to my side and pressed his hand to my back. "What do you say? Time for bed?"

I can't believe we're still alive. I wagged my eyebrows at him. "Best idea I've heard all night."

CHAPTER 23

The next day I followed Niche down a dark abandoned hallway. "Where are we?"

There was not a single student in sight, and I had the overwhelming urge to turn around and go back. Niche's boots clicked on the stone floor as she continued walking. Our entire crew followed behind her, including me. Zinnia was right by my side, and Tuck was next to her as always.

Niche didn't even turn around when she answered. "The library was too crowded with Magtrac exams coming up. I had to think of another place for us to meet to discuss things."

"Still doesn't answer my question."

"This part of the school was built long before New York rose up around it, long before this wing became the cursed wing of the school." She motioned to the cobwebs hanging from the ceiling. "Matteaus shut it down a century ago when it became clear the students were in danger in this specific set of classes."

I held up my hand. "Hold up, so you're bringing us to a side of the school that hasn't been used in a century because it was deemed too dangerous for others and we'll have privacy here? Is anyone else concerned about the fact the plumbing won't be up to date here?"

Grayson chuckled. "Don't worry, love. If you have to pee, I'll pop you over to the loo and get you sorted."

"Ew, I feel so much better now." I rolled my eyes and plucked a spider from the sleeve of my black hoodie. I quickly placed it on the wall and continued following the group through a heavy wooden door.

Niche waved to the torches on the wall. "Tuck, if you would, please."

With the flick of his wrist, he launched four fireballs to each of the torches in the four corners of the room. The floor changed from the stone hallway to a dust-covered green marble. A golden pentacle was inlaid into the marble. It wasn't lost on me that there were five points to that pentacle and five queens. Together, we were strong enough to do anything. But even now, I felt like an outsider, like I didn't belong. The only reason I was here was because of the mark on my shoulder telling the world I was a queen witch. Even my sister didn't want to admit she was my sister. Could I blame her for that? Not really. I'd done some sketchy things in the name of my father.

The rest of the crew filtered into the room. Grayson waved his hand in front of his nose. "It's stale in here. Innit?"

He was right. The air was stale and musty. The tables around the room were all pushed up against the walls and covered in a thick layer of dust. Books were strewn about carelessly, tossed to the side like they'd all left in a hurry.

I ran my finger over the table. "Something scared them into running."

Nova pressed her hand to the wall. "It's a spirit, a restless one at that. But I don't feel any malevolence about it. More like a prankster."

Niche turned around to face us. "We can't be concerned about that today. Now that we have the sword, we can move to the next phase of our plan."

I raised my hand. "Which is?"

"We need to make a potion strong enough to keep a soul safe from actually dying once they reach the heavenly plane." She looked around the room at each of us. "And the ingredients are nearly impossible to find. It's going to take some risky missions to get this done."

"What do we need to get? And where do we have to go?" Tuck pulled a stool out from under a table, brushed it off, then handed it to Zinnia. He grabbed another one and did the same for himself. I wondered if anyone else saw their connection as easily as I did.

Niche held up her fingers, ticking them off one by one. "First, we'll need the sea glass from Poseidon's castle."

I swiped a handful of dust off the closest table, then hopped up to sit on top of it. "Like the kind of glass that's been in the ocean so long it's no longer jagged, but smooth like a crystal?"

Niche nodded. "Exactly that."

"And you want us to go under the ocean to Poseidon's castle?" I glanced around the room at the rest of the crew. "Does no one else think this is a bad idea?"

Niche pulled her glasses off and rubbed at her eyes. "In his bedroom, to be exact."

"What?" I nearly fell off the table.

"You can't be serious." Grayson hopped up next to me and leaned back on his hands. "What if he's in there snogging some sea nymph? That's something I'd rather not see."

Niche held her hand up. "Oh, wait. There's more. We also need to get a golden apple from a tree in Hera's garden. And the only way to do that is to present the dragon with a gift of some sort, to which he will grant you the privilege of answering three riddles. If you're wrong . . . well, you're lunch. If you're correct, then you get the apple."

Ashryn, the noble elf and our quietest knight, spoke up from her perch on top of a bookcase in the back of the room. "What are the riddles?"

"I have no idea." Niche shrugged. "We need the feather of an angel. Oh and, Nova, I have a special job for you."

Tabi chuckled. "That's easy. Follow Matteaus around for a while and collect all the ones he drops."

"We thought that, too. But it has to be feathers from an angel who isn't fallen," I pointed out.

"And how do *you* know that?" Tabi crossed her arms and waved her head back and forth with all the attitude she could muster.

"Because we already tried to get the feathers from him," Zinnia snapped as she narrowed her eyes at Tabi.

Is she defending me? I looked back and forth between the two of them. Tension hung in the air, and no one dared to break the silence.

Finally, Niche cleared her throat. "I get that this is a lot to deal with, but this is your destiny. Now we have a plan. It's time we decide who's going on what mission." She met my gaze. "This is also where you come in. I'll need help with this. The potion has to be exact, or whoever goes to the heavenly plane might not come back down. In which case, we're screwed."

"Well, if you ask me, we're screwed either way." Serrina leaned her hip up against the wall and crossed one leg over the other. "Let's be honest, up until a couple weeks ago, she was playing for the other team. How can we trust her?"

I rolled my eyes. *Not this again . . .*

"I trust her." Nova walked to my side and leaned up against the table. "She's helped us a lot over the past few weeks. There's no reason not to trust her."

"Um . . . hello? Has everyone else here forgotten who her father is?" Serrina jabbed her finger in my direction. "She's literally the spawn of our worst enemy. That counts for something."

"Enough!" Zinnia growled. With her hands curled into fists at her sides, she jumped to her feet. Magic glittered in her wild midnight hair and down her arms.

Tucker reached out and placed his hand on her shoulder. "Zinnia, it'll be all right."

The muscle in her jaw ticked as she spoke through clenched teeth. "It is not all right! Everyone in this room has a problem with O because she is Alataris' daughter. Well, guess what? If you have a problem with her, then you've got a problem with me. Because she's my baby sister."

Boom! It was like a bomb went off in the room. Everyone looked from Zinnia at me and back again. I hopped off the table and walked over to where she stood. I wanted to throw my arms around her to give her a hug, but I held off. "Baby sister, huh?"

She nodded. "That's right."

I turned to stand beside her and faced the rest of the room. My sister, the only family I had left in the world, had just proclaimed me as her family. Pride and a sense of belonging coursed through my chest. I fought not to beam at her. How silly would that look, me with a goofy smile on my face just because she told a handful of people we were related. "I prefer younger. Baby has such a negative feel to it, don't you think . . . sis?"

The corner of her lip twitched. "We'll talk about it later . . . sis."

The room erupted into screams.

Liars!

How could you keep this from us?

What are we going to do now?

They can't be trusted.

How could there be two?

Question after question flew at us. Had we kept a big

secret? Yup. Was it worth the wait? To have my sister tell the world what we were to each other? Absolutely.

I threw my arms up. "Oh, come on, guys. Like Zinnia hasn't saved all your asses before. Like she hasn't gone up against our father time after time showing no fear. Like she hasn't fought for each of you tooth and nail. Just because his blood runs in her veins does not mean she's loyal to him."

Zinnia nodded. "She's right. I've proven myself to you all." She looked down at me. "And so has Ophelia. Tuck and I wouldn't be here without her. She's part of this crew."

"Maybe we should just toss you both out." Serrina shoved away from the wall and came to stand in the middle of the room while glaring at Zinnia.

A sarcastic chuckle burst past my lips. "Boy, smarts really isn't your strong suit, is it, Malibu Barbie? You can't get rid of us because you need us. Hell, we need each other if this is going to work."

"Ophelia's right." Tuck rose and moved next to Niche at the front of the room. "You all might not like what's happening here, but you don't have to like it. We need each other. We need to work together. We have one goal, one enemy, one direction to go in. What other choice do you all have? Give up? Walk away?"

With a huff, Serrina backed away from the middle of

the room and went to her spot leaning up against the wall. "Fine then. Who's going on the first mission?"

Tucker looked right at me, and a half grin tugged at his lips.

Oh crap.

CHAPTER 24

Tabi held her hands beside my ears with her fingers spread out wide. She didn't meet my eye once, nor did she smile or try to make small talk the way she used to.

I waved my hand in front of her face. "Is this how things are going to be with us from now on?"

She pursed her lips. "I don't know what you're talking about." Tabi was the Queen of Elements. Her personality was always bright sunny and full of life. Now she was cold, distant, and could barely look at me. We were standing in the hidden wing of the school dressed in nothing but wetsuits. I felt awkward enough in the thick rubber material that clung to every inch of my body. I didn't need there to be an unspoken tension between us as well. We were heading to face Poseidon and whatever lay in his underwater castle.

"Look, I can't help who my father is."

"It's not that." The air between her hands began to shimmer around my head.

I curled my hands into fists at my sides. "Then what is it?"

"You lied to us all. You knew she was your sister, and you lied. You've done some really great things to help us. It's confusing. Trust isn't easily given, especially to people like us. We've been sent away by our families. We barely have any friends. All because we are the most powerful witches in the world. And there are secrets being kept. It's hard to build confidence in each other when there's no trust." The shimmering around my head stopped, and a perfect bubble formed. She dropped her hands. "There, now you'll be able to breathe underwater."

Guilt sank like a bowling ball in the pit of my stomach. I should've told them all, but how could I? Serrina had reacted exactly as I expected her to. "Well, how do you feel about it?" My voice echoed back at me like I had a fish tank on my head.

"Honestly, I don't know. You didn't exactly give me the chance to think about it the way I should."

She knocked on the top of the bubble. *Tink, tink, tink.*

Now I know what fish at the aquarium feel like.

She placed her hand on my shoulder. "I'll accept it because I have to. But being Alataris' daughters means you two have more to overcome. In the end, will you be able to kill your father?"

I looked her dead in the eyes. "After all he's done, I wouldn't hesitate."

"What about your mom? She's tied to him. A soul mate bond can't be broken."

I fought back the tears that pricked at my eyes when I thought about losing her, how I'd lost her. It felt like a lifetime ago. "We'll cross that bridge when we get to it." I took her hand in mine. "But right now, I need you to please try and forgive me for lying to you. I'm truly sorry. I just didn't know how you guys would react. And let's be honest, some of the crew still haven't accepted it." *One secret down . . . one to go. Tucker.*

Tabi pressed her lips together and nodded. "I get it."

Before I could say anything else, she moved on to the next person in line, forming the bubble around Ophelia's head.

Beckett stepped out in front of us and held up a map contained in a waterproof bag. Though he too wore a wetsuit, his arms were free of the thick material. Bright yellow stripes ran down his sides, and a massive bubble wavered over the top of his head. "Right, so I've never been to Poseidon's castle, obviously. But it is widely known in Evermore that his castle lies hidden in the Bahamas—Andros, to be exact. I've been to the island, so I can portal us onto the beach, and from there Tabi will guide us underwater the rest of the way."

I glanced around, looking for Tuck. "Hey, have you guys seen Tuck?"

"I'm here." His smooth voice came from just behind me. Then he walked around to stand next to Beckett at the front of the room. He was clad only in a pair of swimming trunks, the kind Olympic swimmers wore. They clung to his body from low on his waist all the way to his knees. Every muscle he had was on display, and I couldn't take my eyes off him.

Ophelia jabbed me with her elbow. "You got a little bit of drool right there." She pointed to her lip and laughed.

"Shut up." I elbowed her back.

The cold, dank air in the abandoned wing seeped over my skin, and goose bumps broke out over my arms. I rubbed my hands up and down them while glancing around. "Where's everyone else?"

"Niche and I thought it best if the others helped her ready the potion as the ingredients come in. That way only a few of us are out at a time. She insisted we had Ophelia with us, though. So we get the right ingredients and don't mess this up." Tuck held still as Tabi formed the bubble around his head.

God, he's gorgeous. And all mine. With his dark auburn hair, molten honey eyes, chiseled body, and tan skin, Tucker was hotness on a stick. Add to that his intelligence, protective side, fierce loyalty and I had the world's best soul mate on my hands. How I got so lucky, I didn't know, but there was something positive in this messed up destiny I had, and it was him.

"Um, Zin? You okay?" Tuck's smooth, deep voice broke into my thoughts.

I shook myself, and heat rushed to my cheeks. "Yeah, I'm good."

Beckett held his hands up. "Well, in that case, all aboard." Blue orbs rotated around his fingers, spinning faster and faster until they morphed into one large orb. He threw it a few feet away, and the blue doorway to his portal stood like a perfect oval waiting for us to walk through it.

I gave Ophelia a playful push forward. "After you."

She narrowed her eyes at me over her shoulder. "One day as my sister and you're already being pushy. I don't even know what to do with this."

As we approached the portal, I shoved her through the door even harder. "Tag. You're it!"

Behind me, Tuck chuckled. "Was that necessary?"

"Hey, I've got sixteen years of sisterly torture to make up for. We're at baby steps. Next week I'll steal her favorite pair of shoes."

"Oh, you are bad." The corner of his lip pulled up in that cocky smile I loved so much.

I shrugged. "Lucky for you that I am." I didn't even turn around toward the portal. I simply took a step back and let myself fall through.

CHAPTER 25

TUCKER

One portal ride and a dive into the crystal-clear waters of the Bahamas and we were well on our way to steal something from Poseidon, who ruled the seas the way Matteaus ruled Evermore. Tabi was behind us, using streams of her magic to propel us through the waters straight down toward the underwater castle. Before me stood a large piece of coral. Rainbow colors danced over it, and schools of brightly-colored fish zoomed in and out of all the tiny crevices. I'd forgotten how amazing sea life could be.

Tabi slowed us to a stop just outside an opening in the base of the reef no bigger than one of those tubes kids climbed through on a playground. She pointed toward it. "Don't touch the side. Otherwise . . ." She slid her finger across her throat in a cutting motion.

Greattttt. "I'll go first."

Though our voices were muffled by the bubbles over our heads, I still heard them clearly. I moved in front of Tabi, Zinnia, and Ophelia. I sucked in a deep breath and pushed off the ground. I threw my arms up by my ears and pulled my legs in close together and let my momentum carry me through to the other side. I shot out of the coral tube like a missile from a submarine. One by one, they all followed behind me. The feeling of being weightless and floating in the warm sea eased the sense of dread I had hanging in the pit of my stomach.

I didn't know what we would face or if we'd all come back. I doubted anyone had ever tried to sneak into Poseidon's kingdom to steal something.

Zinnia floated past me with wide eyes. "Oh, wow."

Once Beckett was through, I turned to see what had inspired her awe. I drifted closer to her. "Wow is right."

Sharks, whales, and fish of all different sizes flowed to and from an opulent castle built entirely out of coral and shells. Rays from the sun beamed down through the water to spotlight the half-moon entrance. Glowing fish with tiny neon stripes down their sides swam in straight lines over every hard corner of the castle. Five smaller turrets rose up from the ground. Each one was connected by a wall of coral. Within that wall stood a building that could only be described as the Taj Mahal of the sea. A golden raindrop-shaped roof glinted in the sunlight.

I pointed toward it. "That's where we'll find him."

Zinnia twisted to face me. "How do you know?"

"He's a Greek, and it's the biggest. Where would you think it is?"

"You're right." She kicked her legs and propelled toward the castle. "Come on, let's go."

Together, we swam forward like a school of fish. This time, Tabi didn't use her powers to propel us. We needed to blend in and move at the same pace as the other fish.

Zinnia lifted her hand, and her silver magic gathered in her palm. "So much power. I can feel it."

The water rippled toward her. I knew enough about her to know when she siphoned power and right now, she was feasting on Poseidon's power. Blue sparkles filled her hair and clung to her skin, like she'd rolled in a million crushed blue diamonds. She held her finger up to the side of the bubble around her head and popped it. Zinnia sucked in a deep breath full of water. A wicked smile spread across her face. "Ah, the power of the Greeks feels good. It's spewing out of the castle like a volcano. Like eating pasta then ice cream. I'm all filled up."

A dolphin zoomed by us, spinning and flying under-water. It jetted back toward us, heading straight for Zin. At the last second, it tilted to the side and swam in circles around her body. Her wild midnight hair drifted on the current, and other smaller fish began to gather around her. The dolphin came to a stop beside her, and Zinnia brushed her hand along its flanks, petting it.

"Guys, I have an idea." Zinnia held both her hands out to her sides, and her silver magic poured from her body like rippling radar. "Everyone put your hands out and get ready."

We all did as we were told. I held my hand out, wait-ing. "Um, Zin, why are we—"

"Three, two, one . . . Hold on!" She turned and grabbed onto the dorsal fin of the dolphin next to her. The dolphin took off straight toward the castle.

"Zin! Wait." Another dolphin flew next to me, and I wrapped my hand around its fin and held on. Its skin was smooth like leather and felt as thick as my wetsuit. The water sped past my body, and my legs drifted out behind me. If I hadn't had the bubble over my face, I would've had to close my eyes. Behind me, the others were holding on for dear life as the dolphins carried us straight through the front gates and into the castle. For a split second I saw a large foyer before the dolphins turned and swam us up a winding ramp. Round and round we went, higher and higher into the castle. I was a bird in the land of fish, swimming in circles and going straight up.

The dolphin pulled a hard right turn, and I lost my grip. My body went sailing through the water, and I collided with Zinnia's waiting arms. We drifted back a couple feet before she stopped us. "Whoa there. Are you okay?"

I was twisted and turned on an underwater roller coaster with a never-ending corkscrew. *I'm definitely not okay.* Spinning and dipping in midair was something I'd done all my life, but down here? "Yeah, I'm good."

"You're looking a little green around the gills." Beckett drifted by with his hands behind his head, as if he were lying in bed.

Show-off. "Nah, this bird is all good underwater."

Zinnia waved us toward a set of double doors at the end of the hallway. "This way, guys. I feel something."

Tabi propelled ahead of us and pressed her ear to the door. "I think I hear something."

"You there, stop!" Two hulking mermen raced toward us. Each one had tails like a shark and upper bodies the size of a rhino shifter. They looked like body-builders on steroid times ten. Each of them held a golden trident and pointed it at us as they charged at full speed.

"Tuck, ideas?" Beckett moved to my side.

Ophelia bumped him to the side. "I got this." She raised her hands over her head. "What swims like a shark must now glide in slow motion to the sounds of a harp. Dance and sway with the seaweed above and shower the sea creatures with endless love."

The two guards abruptly stopped and began floating. The sound of a harp filled the air, and they swam around each other, dancing and spinning like the dolphins we'd seen earlier. I held my hands out to my sides and summoned my swords. White-hot power gathered in my palms, and I pictured those long, elegant blades within my grasp. The hilts of my swords filled my hands, and I wrapped my fingers around them. "Good job, O. But you know there'll be more."

Zinnia swam to be beside Ophelia. "What do you want us to do?"

"You guys collect the sea glass. Beckett and I will stand guard." As the words left my mouth, three more mermen swam at a furious rate down the hall toward us. "And, queens?"

They all stopped and looked at me. "Hurry."

I kicked forward, meeting the three mermen head-on. I swung my sword down, blocking a trident from impaling my rib cage. Beckett threw blue orbs at one of the mermen. They stuck together until they formed one big unmovable blob around him. All that stuck out was his head. I pushed off the wall and kicked him square in the chest, or at least where I thought it would be. He drifted back toward the end of the hall, where the blobs expanded to the point of blocking anyone else from getting through.

Beckett wrestled with one of the mermen. They each had two hands on the trident and were grappling for control. A thick shark tail swung toward my face, and I ducked under it. I floated for a moment, losing all my momentum. When his tail came back around, I held my sword in front of my face. I had no leverage as I kicked out as hard as I could. When his tail smacked into my blade, crimson blood clouded the water and I flew backward.

My ass hit the double doors, sending them flying wide-open. The backs of my legs smacked a smooth surface, and I stopped floating. Zinnia, Ophelia, and Tabi all looked at me with wide eyes. "What?"

Zinnia pointed a finger over my shoulder. I turned and came face-to-face with one very pissed off Greek— a pissed off Greek hovering over a seashell the size of a king-sized bed. He crossed his arms over his barrel chest. "What the hell is the meaning of all this?"

Poseidon's eyes wavered from the most vivid to a deep stormy green. His long hair drifted in the water, and the muscle in his jaw flexed. "Well, what are you doing here, Phoenix?"

I twisted my body around and tried to muster up a small bow of respect. But it ended up looking like a failed attempt at a front flip. "Pardon the intrusion, Poseidon. But we have come here for a specific favor."

"Really? Does this have to happen right now?" A beautiful woman snapped from the bed underneath him. She was wrapped in a simmering green blanket. But the blanket didn't cover her from head to toe. In fact, she didn't have toes at all. A delicate blue fish tail hung out from the bottom of the blanket. It flicked back and forth the way an annoyed cat would flick its tail. She studied her long claw-like nails while her lengthy curly hair fanned out around her.

Poseidon held his hand up, silencing her. "Just a moment, my dear."

"Hold up a second." Ophelia moved beside me. "Is she a mermaid?"

The woman rolled her eyes. "Duh."

"Okay, I've been wondering this since I saw the

cartoon about little mermaids. How does it work?" Ophelia's eyes were wide with wonder. "Spare me no detail."

"What the devil are you talking about, little witch?" Poseidon drifted over to a set of mirrors next to the bed. He yanked the door open and pulled out a robe, then jammed his arms into it. Lucky for us he still had his pants on, though I suspected not for long.

"Oh, you know." She winked. "How do mermaids . . . do it? The horizontal mambo, make whoopie, get it on, afternoon delight, buttering the biscuit."

"That's quite enough." Poseidon slashed his hand through the water, and tiny bubbles floated up from the motion. "Weren't you the one who was locked up for all that time by your father?"

"Damn, news travels fast. And yeah, I was locked up, but that didn't mean I lived under a rock. I was out doing shady crap for my dad. I saw things." She crossed her arms.

He gave her a withering look. "Clearly."

When she opened her mouth to say something else, Zinnia's powers wrapped around her waist like a lasso and yanked her back. Zinnia moved up next to me to take Ophelia's place. "My apologies. Ophelia forgot herself."

"Is there an end to this, or are we going to stand here all day?" Poseidon motioned to the mermaid in his bed. "I have guests to tend to."

This is not going well. I cleared my throat. "We've come to ask a favor." He waved me on. "We are in need of a special kind of sea glass only you have. And also perhaps a gift."

Poseidon scoffed and floated down into the bed. "You want me to give you a present after you broke into my castle? Oh, little bird. You ask for a many thing."

"It's not for us," Zinnia blurted, then pressed her lips together before she spoke more softly. "It's for Ladon."

Poseidon perked up. "Hera's dragon, why?"

How much should we reveal to him? How much should we keep secret? If we told him too much, he might want something out of it. Something I wasn't ready to give. I gave Zinnia a sideways glance. She gave me the slightest nod, urging me on. "We need a golden apple from one of the trees in Hera's garden."

Poseidon shook his head and chuckled. "I do hope one of you is smart enough." He rose to his feet and clapped his hands together. "And what of you, little siphon witch. I see my power suits you."

Zinnia inclined her head. "It rolls off of you in waves, and yet I'm sure you felt nothing from me."

"Indeed, I did not." He sucked in a deep breath. "I will help you. But it will cost you."

We were running out of time. We had to get to the crown before Alataris made any more moves on the city —or anywhere else for that matter. I didn't want to agree to anything, but what choice did I have? I ground my teeth together. "Name it."

"One of you will stay here with me for the next two days. As my guest. We have much to discuss, and I wish all my questions to be answered fully."

"How do I know you will guarantee the safety of whoever stays?" But who would I leave behind? Each and every member of our team was necessary.

"I give you my word that whoever stays will be safely returned to Evermore Academy in two days' time. Unharmed and unaltered in any way." He extended his hand out to me.

"I'll stay." I extended my hand out toward his when a current of water knocked me sideways. My feet were above my head and I drifted along the way an astronaut did in space.

Tabi rushed up and took Poseidon's hand. "No, I will stay."

I kicked my legs out and swung my arms to swim beside her. I grabbed her shoulder and pulled her back.

The others closed in around us. We stood in a small huddle. "Tabi, you don't have to do this."

"Yes, I do. If something happens, I will be the only one who can get out of here alive besides Zinnia, and you need her for the next stages of our mission." She looked me dead in the eyes. "Do not forget I am a queen of elements, and that includes water. I am comfortable here. I don't even need a bubble to breathe. You can't say the same. None of you can. I am doing this for us."

What she said made sense. "But it is my duty to protect you."

"Right now, it's our duty to protect the world. I got this." She had all the confidence in the world. Her face was calm and smooth and shined with the blue tints of the sea.

"Thank you, Tabi." Zinnia wrapped her up in a hug. "We will be together in no time."

"I look forward to it." Tabi offered her a half smile.

I spun around to face Poseidon. "You have a deal."

"Excellent." He held his hand out and snapped his finger. Fragments of blue and green sea glass dropped down from his ceiling into the palm of his hand. Piece by piece, they fell like snowflakes until there was a small pile sitting in his palm.

"You had sea glass in the ceiling over your bed? See, I knew you all get down and dirty here." Ophelia threw her arms up and spun around in a circle, swishing her legs the way a fish might.

Poseidon rolled his eyes. "As for the gift, I happen to know Ladon will be interested in this." He reached up to the silver-plated necklace hanging off his shoulders and plucked a blue pearl the size of a golf ball from it.

Beckett held his hand out and opened a small portal in the center of his hand. "Just drop it in here."

"Where's it going?" I had to be sure that after we came all this way, the supplies we needed were reaching where they needed to be.

Beckett's lips quirked. "I'm sure Niche will love to have this dumped on her desk."

I chuckled. "What a pleasant surprise."

Poseidon tilted his hand to the side and let the contents slide into the hole of nothingness, all but the pearl. Beckett scooped it up a moment before it too went into the portal. Poseidon looked Beckett up and down. "Young warlock, you have much to tell. Are you sure you would not prefer to stay?"

Beckett shook his head. "My secrets will remain my own, thanks."

"Pity." He held his hand up, and the windows to his bedroom flew open. "Now, if our business is concluded . . ."

A beam of water smacked into my chest and sent me

flying out the window and out of his castle. The bubble around my head popped, and I sucked in a gasping breath of saltwater. My lungs filled with the burning liquid, and I struggled for the surface. But there was none. We were hundreds of feet below. Black dots swarmed my vision, and a moment before I lost it all, the only thing I could think was, *Oh crap. I'm going to die.*

CHAPTER 26

My body tumbled end over end and rolled with the waves. I flipped over, and my shoulder struck into the ocean floor. I twisted and kicked straight up. My head breached the surface. I sucked in a gasping breath a second before I was hit with another wave and dragged back under. Saltwater burned up my throat and into my eyes. I swung my arms out and kicked my legs, fighting the crashing waves. I was thrown forward, and I teetered on the shoreline once more. When the tide rushed back out, I hunched on all fours and crawled in the shallow waves. I sucked in deep, heaving breaths and coughed up the water and sand stuck in my throat.

Waves smacked into me, and I fell flat on my stomach. I rolled over onto my back and spread my arms out wide. Tangles of my hair stuck to my neck and cheeks. The sand cushioned the back of my head, and I pressed my hands to my stomach. *Still alive!* When I peeked my eyes open, I looked up at the dark sky. The moon was full and closer than I'd ever seen it. The stars sparkled like diamonds in the dark, and a warm breeze wafted over me. If I hadn't almost died, I might actually like this place. I glanced at my side, expecting to see Tuck, Ophelia, and Beckett. But no one was there.

I climbed to my feet and cupped my hands around my mouth. "Tuck!"

Silence. I spun around, and my pulse raced in my veins. "Ophelia!"

Nothing. *Shit, shit, shit.* "Beckett!"

The last of Poseidon's powers resonated in my system, and I clapped my hands together, drawing them to the forefront. I closed my eyes and tried to zero in on their powers. Ophelia's dark purple danced behind my eyes. Beckett's royal blue glowed right next to her. And Tuck's crimson energy was zooming around them both. *What the hell?*

Tuck hurled from the water like a bullet. He held a limp Beckett in one hand and an unconscious Ophelia in the other. His wings were barely flapping, and they all looked like drowned animals. Tuck was soaked from head to toe, and his eyes were half-lidded with exhaustion. He spun in a circle. The fire wings lit up the night sky and the water below him. He looked like an avenging angel . . . my angel. He turned around and bellowed, "Zinnia!"

I threw my hands up into the air and waved them back and forth. "I'm here!"

His head snapped up, and the moment his eyes met mine, he sucked in a deep breath. He shoved his shoulders back and began flying toward me. My heart slowed to a manageable pace, and I stepped back into the water. It ran over my toes, and I bent over to place my hand in the water. I threw the last of Poseidon's powers out into the ocean.

"Drop them."

"What?" He struggled to hold both of them at the same time. Beckett was the same size as Tuck, and Ophelia was only slightly smaller than me. Both of them were soaked and dead weight with their wetsuits on. Even from where I stood on the shore, which at least fifty feet away, I spotted his white-knuckle grip on the two of them. He hovered over the rough sea, fighting to get everyone to safety.

While the waves continued to pound the beach, I smoothed out a small portion, like a slide right underneath Tuck. "Drop them. I promise they'll be okay."

Tucker let go of Beckett first. He dropped down onto the slide. It cushioned him the way a pillow would, and then the water carried him toward the shoreline. He never sank down below the surface. He merely floated over it. Next, Tuck dropped Ophelia. She fell onto the slide the same way Beckett had. This time, Tuck flew above her, staying with her until she washed up next to me.

I dropped down to her side and pulled her head into my lap. "What's happened to her?"

Tuck fell to his knees next to me and placed his hands on his thighs. Drops of water dripped from his face onto the sand. He shoved his hand into his hair, pushing it back out of his face. "I think she's exhausted. She nearly drowned, Zin. We all did." He placed his hand on my shoulder. "I lost sight of you. I'm so sorry."

"It's all right." I looked at the sky and out over the water. I didn't recognize anything. Even the stars looked unfamiliar. "I didn't think Hera's garden would be this close to Poseidon's castle."

Tuck shook his head. "It isn't. I'm pretty sure that shot of water he threw at us sent us into some kind of underwater portal. If he had just carried us back to shore, we'd still be in the Bahamas. And this isn't the Bahamas, I can tell you that much."

"So we were in a water portal? Seriously?"

"I'm pretty sure. We could be on the other side of the world for all we know." Tuck placed his hand on my shoulder and gave it a little squeeze. "Are you okay, though? You're not hurt?"

"I'm okay. I made it to shore just fine." And by fine, I meant only a couple of bumps and bruises. I brushed the hair from Ophelia's face. "O, come on. You gotta wake up."

Her eyes fluttered wildly, then her eyes slid back shut.

Tuck squeezed my shoulder. "Don't worry. She just needs to rest."

I shook my head. "I don't think we have time for that."

When I looked farther inland and away from the ocean, a wall of ivy rose up in front of us. Beyond the dense ivy, palm trees swayed in the breeze and gigantic tropical flowers peeked up over the edge of the wall. But in the distance, in the dead center of it all, was a towering tree the size of a redwood. The bright blue moonlight glinted off the golden apples hanging from the oversized branches. Wait. Were those apples or basketballs . . .? Apples the size of basketballs?

"Maybe I can just fly up and grab one and we can get out of here?" Tuck stood up straight and took a step toward the wall. An ear-splitting roar stopped him dead in his tracks.

Beckett limped next to him. "I'd say that's a hardcore no entry warning." He pressed his fingers to his side and winced. "Remind me that next time there's an underwater mission with Poseidon, I'm out. That dude almost drowned me twice already."

"Are your ribs okay?" I wanted to stand up and check them, but Ophelia was still out cold in my lap.

Beckett's brow furrowed, and he pursed his lips. "Yeah, it's just a cramp in my side."

The leaves of the wall rustled, and the wall upheaved like a shockwave was going through the ground. I looked down at Ophelia. "We definitely don't have time for this. Sorry, guys. I need to borrow some of your powers."

Before they answered, I grabbed onto their wrists and let my magic take over. They each fell to their knees beside me. I was careful to take the smallest amount possible. I dropped my grip and held my hand over Ophelia's chest.

"That stings." Beckett lumbered to his feet.

Tuck leaned in and whispered, "A little warning next time, my love."

Goose bumps skidded over my skin at his words, and I fought not to smile. My magic fell from my hand into

Ophelia's chest. She shot straight up like I'd injected her heart with adrenaline. She sucked in gasping breaths, and her eyes were wide with shock.

She pressed her hands to her face and body. "What happened? Am I dead? Did we all die?"

"Not yet, my dear. But there's still time tonight," a deep voice hissed.

All at once, our heads snapped up, and I sat with an ancient dragon hovering over me, its teeth dripping with saliva. It ran its tongue over its lips the way a dog would before it devoured a bone. The dragon was nothing like the dragon I'd rescued from Alataris. No, this one was a vibrant Everest green, with a long, flat head and a thin, snake-like physique. Its arms and legs stuck out from its body. Each one bent at ninety-degree angles at the elbow and went straight toward the ground. Razor-sharp talons tipped its hands. Bat-like wings jutted out from his front arms. Each one was bright green with red markings across them.

I rose to my feet and extended my hand out toward Beckett. "Give me the pearl."

The golf ball sized pearl filled my hand. I lifted it above my head, presenting it to the dragon. "Great Ladon, we come with this gift for you."

The dragon darted forward, slithering over the ground like a millipede but ten times faster. He twisted his head around, studying the pearl with quick, twitchy movements. "This is from the sea god Poseidon."

I didn't have the nerve to correct him and tell him Poseidon was no god, though his power felt that way. I nodded. "Yes, he gave it to us himself. He said if we presented this to you, it would be an acceptable gift in exchange for one golden apple."

Ladon tilted his head all the way back and looked at the giant redwood tree. In a blur of activity, he spun around and snatched the pearl from my hand and was ten feet away. His black claws stood out against it. He whipped his tail toward the center of the garden. "The gift you have brought to me will gain you entrance to the garden. Whether or not you leave with the apple . . ." He darted back in front of my face. One moment he was so far ahead of me, and now we stood nose to nose. His tongue darted out and brushed my temple. "Well, that's up to the intelligence you all carry."

Tuck curled his hands into fists at his sides, and the muscle in his jaw ticked. "Please lead the way."

"Jealousy does not become usssssss." Ladon darted away from me and through an archway in the ivy wall. "Come along."

His words drifted on the wind like a hypnotic whisper I was compelled to follow. My feet sank into the sand as I marched behind him. Tuck, Beckett, and Ophelia flanked my sides, each of us walking in silence through Hera's garden. Pools of water were spread throughout the grounds. Each one held all different kinds of floating lilies. Golden pixies fluttered about, leaving trails of gold dust in their wake. They reminded me of the ones at Evermore Academy, except they seemed much quieter and calmer.

Topiaries of giant cats and dogs chased each other through the winding paths of the garden. Flowers of all shapes and colors lined the pathways and filled the open areas. Their fragrant scents mixed with the smell of the sea. The white sand was so soft under my toes that it felt like I was walking on cotton balls. I glanced up at the stars once more, not recognizing a single constellation. "Does anyone know where in the world we are?"

Beckett shook his head. "Unlike Poseidon, this place isn't on any map. We're lucky he just blasted us here. Otherwise, it could've taken years for us to find this place."

Tuck moved so close to me his shoulder brushed mine and a warm tingling ran through my body. "The question is once we get what we came here for, are we going to be able to leave?"

Beckett opened his fingers, and a small orb formed in the center of his palm then fizzled out. "This is going to be interesting."

"Did I do that?" *Crap.* I didn't realize I took that much power from him.

"Nah, you barely took anything. I didn't even feel it." His eyes darted to the side, and he whispered, "There's some kind of old magic here preventing me from making a portal."

I opened my powers and let them flow over my skin. I got half a glimmering sheen on my hands, then nothing happened. "Crap."

"Yup." Ophelia held her fingers out in front of me. "I got nothing."

Tuck held his hand behind his back. A moment later, the tip of his sword jutted up between his shoulder blades then back down again. "At least I can still summon my weapons."

As we neared the center of the garden, I looked up and up and up at the towering redwood tree. Its trunk was as thick as the hull of a plane. The roots extend out over the ground in a tangled web that disturbed the white sand and flowers around it. Thick green vines wound up the trunk of the tree, and large hibiscus flowers bloomed over the vines and trunk. The canopy was made of leaves the size of beach balls. Those glinting golden apples made me want to reach up and try to pluck one, even though they were at least fifty feet in the air. Each one rotated in place like a spinning globe.

Ladon twisted his body around the base of the tree trunk. His glowing red eyes narrowed and zoomed in on me. "Now then, little witch. Your token has bought you the opportunity to solve three riddles. Should you do so, the golden apple is yours. Though I should warn you, I have yet to give up a single apple."

"Well, perhaps you're feeling generous?" I put on my best smile. We were trapped, didn't know where we were, and there was a dragon who looked ready to devour us at a moment's notice. A moment of weakness could cost us everything.

His forked tongue slipped from between his lips. "Not likely."

"All right, Toothless, let's get this party started." Ophelia put her hands on her hips.

Tuck, Beckett, and I all gaped at her. How could she be so blasé about the situation we were in? I jabbed my elbow into her side. "What are you doing?"

"Oh, come on. Isn't it obvious? Either we answer the riddles the right way, or he's going to eat us." She turned back toward Ladon. "Isn't that right?"

"Well, maybe not you. Attitude does taste a bit sour on the tongue." He unfurled himself from the tree and leaned up against it in a crouch. "But the rest of you will do just fine. I've always liked the taste of fowl."

Tucker cleared his throat. "Did you just call me an entree?"

"If the bird fits in the pan, then pluck it."

I tapped my foot with impatience. We didn't have an eternity to get the ingredients for the potion. Time was of the essence. We needed to get the sword blessed, we needed to get the crown, and we needed to take down Alataris once and for all. "Enough of this. Give us your riddles, and we'll solve them and be on our way."

He slammed the side of his body into the tree. Leaves fluttered to the ground, and one single apple dropped down. Before it hit the sand, Ladon whipped his tail forward and caught it. He coiled the tip of it around the apple and held it up next to his face. "Brave wordsssss, little witch. You sure it's worth it?" He waved the apple back and forth.

"Ask your questions." Tuck laid his hand on my shoulder. His warm touch seeped into my cool skin, and I wanted to move closer to him, to wrap my arm around his waist and curl into the side of his body. Instead, I stood still as a statue, wishing I could do more in front of everyone else, but not making a move to do so.

"Fine. We shall start off with something easy." He

flopped over onto his back and held the apple between his two claws, tossing it from one hand to the other. "I have oceans, lakes, and rivers, but no water. I have cities, streets, and bridges, but no houses. I have mountains, but no trees. I have landmarks, but no statues. What am I?"

"What in the hell does any of that mean? You can't have an ocean and no water." Ophelia stepped forward and raised her fist at him. "What are you playing at?"

I grabbed her elbow and yanked her back. "What is wrong with you?"

She tilted her head to one side and cracked her neck, then did the same on the other side. "I have no idea. There's too much testosterone magic in my body. I just want to punch something . . . well, more than I usually do."

Tucker moved to stand in front of us. He gave Ladon his back and formed a small huddle with the four of us. "We need to think here. What could possibly have every single one of these things but have nothing at the same time?"

I was at a total loss, and this was supposed to be the easy one. *Screwed, we are so screwed.* Ophelia mumbled the lines over and over again.

A deep chuckle sounded from the dragon. "If you can't solve this one, I hate to see what you'd do with the rest. Wait, no. I take it back. I'd love it."

Tuck snapped his fingers, and a smirk tugged at his lips. "I think I got it. You're a map!"

I froze, waiting for Ladon to react in some way. I could almost picture him opening his mouth over my body to swallow me whole. "Maybe next time we should conference about our answers?"

Ophelia cupped her hand around her mouth and mumbled to us, "If there is a next time."

"Have a little faith, ladies." Tucker threw his shoulders back and looked Ladon dead in the eye. "I'm right. What's the next riddle?" He beamed with confidence, and damn if it wasn't the hottest thing.

The dragon's forked tongue darted from its mouth two more times before he gave a single nod. "Well done, Phoenix. But don't get too excited. I still have a hankering for fried phoenixxxxxx."

"Ew." I wrinkled my nose and shook my head.

Ladon rose up high on his tail and hovered over us. "What is greater than the Creator, eviler than Lucifer himself, the poor have it, the rich need it, and if you consume it, you'll die?"

I pressed my hands to the sides of my head and rubbed my temples in a circular motion. I shifted from one foot to the other. Once again, Tuck and Beckett moved in closer so we huddled in a small circle.

Ophelia bit her bottom lip. "I can't think of anything

greater than the Creator or eviler than Lucifer. I mean, my dad is pretty evil, but he's not the devil. Maybe it has something to do with the Greeks?"

Tuck nodded. "I think because we are in Hera's garden, there's a possibility it has to relate to the Greeks. They are an arrogant bunch, after all. They could think something is more powerful than the Creator. And there are lots of things that could kill you if you eat them."

"Yes, but is there something the poor have and the rich need that the Greeks are related to?" I rubbed my temples even harder. How could our potion rely so much on a single answer? This was life or death. The fate of Evermore rested on our response.

Beckett shook his head. "I got nothing."

Oh . . . my . . . God! I slapped Tuck in the arm. His shoulder jostled back. "That's it!"

He righted himself and smiled. "What's it?"

"Nothing! The answer is literally *nothing*. What's greater than the Creator? Nothing. What's eviler than Lucifer himself? There is nothing eviler than the devil. What do the poor have? Nothing. What do the rich need? Nothing. And if you eat nothing, you will die. The answer is nothing." My hands shook, and a smile spread across my face. "I'm right. I know it."

Ophelia motioned toward the dragon. "Throw it out there. Let's see if we get eaten."

I turned around to face Ladon. The dragon leaned up against the side of the tree. That golden apple was still in its coiled tail. I sucked in a deep breath and squeezed my eyes shut for a second. "You're nothing."

He pressed his claw to his chest. "Me? I'm nothing?" He threw his head back with all the drama of the best actors. "How insulting. I should make you my dessert just for that."

I didn't have time for this. I crossed my arms. "I'm right, though, aren't I?"

"Ugh, yesssss." If he had eyelids or could roll those dark glassy eyes, he would. As it was now, he settled for all the sarcasm he could manage. "I don't think you'll be as smart for the last one."

"Let's have it then." Ophelia waved him on with all the impatience of a two-year-old.

How could it be that we stood in one of the most beautiful gardens in all the world and every single one of us wanted to leave? The stars reflected in each of the pools surrounding us, the air smelled of sweet nectar, and the sand was satin under my feet. Flowers of every shape and color I could think of surrounded us, pixies danced in the blue moonlight, and I couldn't wait to get the hell out of here. Clearly, neither could Ophelia.

"Very well, tiny loud witch." He tossed the apple up into the air with his tail and caught it with his talons.

Then to my surprise, he balanced it on one long claw and spun it, the way a pro basketball player would spin a ball. "Now do pay attention, and I warn you. You'd better think twice. Many a mortal has failed in this last one. What four-letter word ends in K and means the same thing as intercourse?"

A bark of laughter burst from Ophelia. "Who would've thought our dragon was a perv. That's easy. Fu—"

I threw my hand over her mouth. "Stop!"

Ladon shot straight up and hovered just over us. "What did she say?"

"Talk. She said the answer is talk." Beckett walked up behind Ophelia and wrapped his arms around her torso.

The dragon shook his head. "That is not what I heard." His tongue darted from his mouth in three quick successions. Was he tasting my fear on the air? "Oh, you silly little mortalsss. You always fall for that one. Your dirty little minds have won me many a meal."

I pushed Ophelia behind me and started to back away. Tuck and Beckett flanked my sides as we moved in a small group. Beckett held his hand out, trying to form his orb, only to get nothing but a bit of blue mist that blew away on the breeze. "Maybe if we get to the beach."

Shit, shit, shit. The beach was at least a hundred yards

away. How would we make it a whole football field away without getting eaten? And even then, would Beckett be able to make a portal to get us back to the Academy? Tucker's shoulder brushed against mine, and that one second of contact was all I needed to swallow my fear down and face what was about to happen.

Tuck cleared his throat. "The answer is talk. You know it, and we know it. So if you'll please give us the apple, we will gladly be on our way."

Ladon tossed the apple back to catch it with his tail. It coiled around the golden sphere as he slithered forward. His arms and legs moved over the ground like a spider, and his body swayed from side to side like a snake. He was only a few feet away from us now. "Leaving so sssssooonnnn? I think not. She answered wrong, and now you must pay the price."

He lunged forward with his mouth wide-open. Teeth the size of my entire body flipped down from his upper lip. They glistened with thick saliva. *Poison?* I didn't want to stick around to find out. Beckett yanked Ophelia to the side at the same time Tuck pulled me to the other side of the path. Ladon darted right past us. His long, scaly body glistened like the smoothest leather. Sand flew up as he twisted his body back to face us.

Becket and Ophelia stood on one side of the path, and we were on the other. Tuck pointed to the winding walkway behind them. "Run. We'll meet you on the beach. Be ready."

"The apple?" Beckett grabbed Ophelia's hand.

I summoned my magic to my hands. It wasn't as strong as it normally was, but it was there. "We'll get it. Just be ready to leave."

"I'm not leaving without you." Ophelia yanked against Beckett's grip.

"O! I will be there. Just get the portal open. I promise." I gave her a nod of encouragement.

"Okay, but if you don't make it there, I swear I'm going to kill you and steal all your clothes." She let Beckett drag her away. "Be careful."

With one hand, I held my magic. With the other, I summoned my blade. There was a flash of white light in the corner of my eye. Tuck summoned his blades. "You ready for this?"

I shook my head. "No, but let's do it anyway."

"I'll get the apple." He stepped out in front of me. "You distract him as best as you can."

I nodded. "Don't die."

"You neither." He winked at me, then took off running at the beast head-on.

Ladon roared and rushed forward. The ground shook under my feet. He opened his mouth, going straight for Tuck's torso. At the last second, Tuck flipped up and over the dragon's head. He landed in a crouch on its back, then darted toward the apple coiled within its tale. He dragged his sword down the dragon's back as he ran. Ladon reared up and tossed around like a bucking bull.

Now was my chance. I pumped my arms and ran at him full speed. Ladon's eyes locked on me, and he twisted violently. His mouth snapped just over my head as I dropped to my knees and skidded under his body.

I jumped up and threw my magic right into his chest. It exploded, leaving a scorch mark on his green scales. I turned to the side and ran toward one of his arms and slashed my blade into his wrist just above his claws. His skin was so thick I broke it only enough to leave a deep cut. He dropped down onto his stomach, pinning my legs beneath him.

"Got the apple?" I screamed.

"Almost," Tuck called back.

I clawed at the ground, trying to pull myself free. Sweat ran down the sides of my face, and sand clung to my skin and neck. I didn't want to tell Tuck I was trapped. We needed the damn apple more than I needed to be free at this exact second.

"Where are you, little witch? Magic will be a good appetizer before my main entree." Ladon coiled around, searching for me. His wing and twisted body blocked me from his view. I pulled at the ground even harder. Sand caked under my fingernails, and blood ran from the palms of my skin.

"Need a hand?" Tuck stood over me with the apple tucked under one of his arms.

"Ugh, yeah." I reached my hand up toward him.

"So quiet, little mortals. Are you scared?" he purred. "Of course you are. I can taste it in the air. It's the sweet-eesssst ssssmmmeell of all." Ladon held still, waiting for us to reveal ourselves.

Tuck handed me the apple and held up three fingers. Then two. Then one. He shoved his sword into Ladon's side. It went clean through his skin all the way to the hilt. Blood streaked down his side and dripped onto me. He contorted in pain and roared. It was all the movement I needed to get free. I hurried to my feet and ran behind him straight toward the beach.

Tuck was hot on my heels. "Go faster, Zin."

My breaths heaved in my chest, and the muscles in my legs burned as I sprinted out toward the entrance. The ivy wall rose up before me, and the archway was only a few more yards away. Behind me, Ladon crashed through the garden, knocking over trees and fountains. Water exploded from every direction. I ducked, dodging the debris that flew over my head. On the edge of the beach, Beckett stood holding a wavering portal wide-open. His skin was pale, and sweat covered him from head to toe.

Ophelia's eyes widened as she waved toward the portal. "Don't look back. Just keep coming. Keep running!"

Don't look back? I glanced over my shoulder. Ladon was gaining on us. Blood coated his body, and he snarled widely. "Get in. I'm right behind you."

Ophelia shook her head. Three more steps and I was at her side. I shoved the apple into her hand. "Take this."

"What?" She wrapped her hands around it.

I kicked my leg out and shoved her forward with both hands, tripping her into the portal. She fell forward into the blue pool, disappearing from my sight. At least she was safe, and the apple would be at Evermore Academy where it had to be. I turned around, holding my blades at the ready. Tuck tackled me by wrapping his arms around my waist. I fell backward into the portal. The blue pool swarmed the sides of my vision.

Ladon leapt at the shrinking opening. At the last second, Beckett jump in front of him. I reached over Tuck's back and grabbed onto Beckett's hand, yanking him forward. The portal shrank down behind him. Ladon's snout smacked into it. His tongue shot out and wrapped around Beckett's ankle. I held on with everything I had as he pulled us back toward the surface. My heart hammered in my chest as the world swirled around me. The portal closed, cutting off Ladon's tongue. The last thing I heard was his pained roar as we fell back into oblivion.

I closed my eyes and let go.

CHAPTER 27

ZINNIA

We shot out of the portal one right after the other, landing in a football pile on the cold hard stone hallways of Evermore Academy. Ophelia was smooshed under me.

"Seriously, you tripped me into a portal?" She shoved her hands into the floor and tried to push us off her.

Tucker and Beckett were both piled on top of me, and I felt like the cheese in a grilled cheese sandwich—completely melted and drooping tired. I sucked in a deep sigh. "Someone had to go first."

"Ah, ah, ah. Shit!" Beckett leapt up off us and kicked his leg out, shaking it wildly. There wrapped around his ankle was the forked part of Ladon's tongue, still twitching and writhing.

I scooted back against the wall. "Ew. Get it off."

"What do you think I'm trying to do?" Beckett bent down and grabbed two sides of the forked tongue and peeled them away from his leg. "It won't come off."

"You trust me, bro?" Tucker stood next to him, studying the tongue.

"Yeah, do what you gotta do." Beckett held his leg out. I felt like I was about to watch a YouTube video of two guys about to do something entirely stupid.

Tuck held his hand out, and fire shot from his palm like a flame thrower. He hit the tongue dead-on. Beckett's arms pinwheeled, and he fell back on his ass. "Don't light me on fire."

"You said you trusted me." Tuck shrugged.

I was just waiting for one of them to scream *hold my beer and watch this.*

The tongue turned to a pile of ash below Beckett's leg, and he scrambled back, patting the bottom of his wetsuit. "You didn't burn me."

"Psh, don't sound so surprised." Tuck turned around to face Ophelia and me. "Are you all right?"

I nodded. "Yeah, I'm okay."

"I'm good, too. Even though she pushed me." Ophelia crossed her arms over her chest, and her lips pulled down into a frown.

"Oh, please. I'm pretty sure you fell . . . I've seen you

walk." I chuckled and shoved her in the shoulder playfully.

Tuck pressed his hand to his mouth as his shoulders vibrated with his suppressed laughter.

Beckett stood, looking in any direction but right at us. His lips pulled up into a smile. "I think I'll take the apple to Niche."

I glanced around the school. "Guys, what's going on here?"

Tuck followed my gaze. "What do you mean?"

"The school is silent. No students, no chatter, not even the pixies are out. What's going on?" I looked at the sky. The sun was just rising, and it was the next day back in New York. Even this early in the morning there was usually some activity. I didn't know where Hera's garden was, but I knew it had to be on the other side of the world, or maybe not in this world at all. Even so, back at school had to be no earlier than five in the morning.

Tuck spun in a slow circle. "You're right. Something's up."

Heavy footsteps thundered toward us. I gathered my magic in my hands, ready to siphon whatever power they had. Beside me, Tuck summoned his swords, and Beckett held his glowing blue orbs dancing between his fingers. The footsteps came to a halt at the end of the hallway, and I held my hands up.

"Cross?" Ophelia ran toward him and threw herself into his arms. Then she took an awkward step back from him and cleared her throat. She swiped her long hair behind her ears, and her eyes darted toward us. "Um, what are you doing here?"

"What am I doing here? What are you guys doing here?" He started running down the hall toward the courtyard. "We need to get going."

Ophelia took off running by his side and we followed quickly behind him. We were all still in our wetsuits, barefoot, and covered in sand. Ladon's dragon blood dried down my arm and across my wetsuit in crimson rivets. This was madness. We were running from one thing to the next.

I was exhausted, starving, and in need of a shower. "Where are we going?"

Cross waved us forward. "Come on. It was Grayson and Serrina's idea."

"What was?" I slowed my pace as we came upon Grayson and Serrina hiding behind one of the columns around the courtyard.

"Shhhhh." Serrina pressed her finger to her lips and waved for us to get down.

I dropped to my stomach and crawled out to her. "What the hell is going on?"

Serrina hunkered down. "We're getting the angel feather."

"What? How?" Tuck crawled out next to me. He was still wearing only his wetsuit swim trunks. His chest was bare and covered in dirt and grime. The smell of the ocean clung to my hair and skin. I was caked in sticky crap and wasn't the slightest bit ready for what was about to happen.

Serrina pointed out to the middle of the courtyard. Tuck and I peeked around the column and froze.

I jumped to my feet. "Niche."

Grayson grabbed my wrist and pulled me back into place. "You want to ruin the whole bloody thing, go right ahead. But we have a plan. Just stay put."

Niche lay in the middle of the courtyard. Her body was lifeless. The color leeched from her cheeks, and a cold blue tone tinged her lips. Her chest didn't rise and fall with breath, and her eyes were closed tightly. I wanted to race out to her but kept my head down. "What happened to her?"

"She took a potion called sleeping death or something like that." Serrina sat still as a statue.

Ophelia wrapped her hand in Serrina's shirt and

yanked her up, so they were nose to nose. "What do you mean she took sleeping death?"

"Um, take it easy. She knows what she's doing." Serrina plucked Ophelia's fingers from her white button-down shirt one by one.

Ophelia turned to Cross. "We need to get to the lab now."

"Take the apple." I pointed toward it. "For safe-keeping."

Without hesitation, Cross extended his hand out to her. She took it, and he yanked her to her feet. They ran down the hall and out of sight. I couldn't take my eyes off Niche. How could we have only been gone for a couple hours and this happened? "Look, you need to tell me exactly what this plan is, because from where I'm sitting, this isn't a good one."

"Right, so it's like this, love. We give Niche the sleeping death potion, and when the Angel of Death comes to reap her soul, we sneak up and pluck one of his feathers. Then we wake Niche up. Boom. Bang. Done. And we've got ourselves a sodding feather." Grayson sat back against the wall with his hands behind his head, looking so pleased with himself.

Tuck pinched the bridge of his nose. "How about the fact that the Angel of Death is invisible to us? How are we going to steal a feather from him if we can't see him?"

Grayson and Serrina both pointed toward the roof. Matteaus walked across the pointed rooftop of the school. His wings were spread wide, and his chest was bare. When he turned his back to us, a long black tattoo ran from the back of his neck down between his wings and ended at the waistband of his leather pants. He had his two swords strapped across his back. "He's just going to engage him a bit to distract him."

My mouth dropped open. "Are you all insane? You're going to attack the Angel of Death?"

"Right-o. Also, don't let his scythe touch you. If it even nicks your skin, your soul will leave your body." Grayson still didn't move. He looked so calm, so casual.

"Oh, is that all?" I wanted to smack him. This was a serious mission, and he was lounging around like he was on vacation. I met Tuck's gaze. "Are they serious?"

"Apparently." Tuck rolled his shoulders and narrowed his eyes. "I'm going to back Matteaus up."

"You heard what they said. You can't even let that ax on steroids thing touch you. Not even a paper cut." I wanted to pull him in close to me, to kiss him and hug him just for a moment before he risked his life again. For days, we'd been risking our lives to collect ingredients for the potion with no break in between.

"I know." When I looked into his molten honey eyes, I knew he wanted to say more, to be open about us in front of everyone. Our lives could end at any moment, and we were spending what little time we had hiding who and what we were to each other.

Grayson cleared his throat. "Brace yourselves. It's about to happen."

My heart leapt up into my throat, and I wanted to reach out and hold Tucker by my side. But this was the life we were born into, what we were meant to be. I watched as Matteaus crouched down low and spread his wings out wide. Still, there was no action or movement around Niche. What did he see that I couldn't? Matteaus leapt straight up into the air, then he pulled his wings in tight and dive-bombed right at Niche. A moment before he would smash into her, his body twisted in the opposite direction. The ground exploded beneath him, and he punched down into the crater. His fists were a blur of motion, and his face was a mask of anger. It was like a spell lifted off Matteaus' prey or he beat it off of him. But we could all make out a hooded figure beneath him,

His body went airborne and slammed into one of the stone columns. It cracked, and pieces of rock rained down on him. "Come out."

The hooded figure rose out from the crater. His black robes billowed in the wind. The man drew his hood back from his face. His skin glowed with an ethereal shimmer I could barely comprehend. An array of rainbow light illuminated the ground around him, and his silvery hair flowed back from his head in a perfect widow's peak down to his waist. His face was regal, with a long straight nose, high cheekbones, and full plump lips. "Matteaus, this is not the path you are to be on."

Matteaus drew his swords and held them at his sides. "What do you know of my path?"

"Kane will hear of this." The angel threw his cloak off his shoulders and let it fall to the ground. He spread his shining white wings. Golden armor covered him from his neck down to his feet. It wasn't the kind you'd see in medieval times. No, this was thinner and moved with him like a second skin. It didn't clatter or clank when he moved.

"My God," I whispered.

The angel's head whipped in my direction, and I ducked down lower. Matteaus stomped forward. "You can't have this one."

"That is not for you to decide." He spun his scythe in his hand. The long blade glinted in the light of the rising sun.

"Actually, it is." Matteaus launched off the ground. He held his swords high up over his head and extended his body to its full length as he brought them down onto the angel. The sound of clashing metal echoed around the halls.

"That's my cue." Grayson shot to his feet and darted forward with his vampire speed. He headed straight toward those glowing white wings. One more foot and he'd be there. The angel spun in a circle and threw his wings out wide. One wing smacked into Grayson's chest, sending him flying across the courtyard, through one of the archways, and right into the hard stone wall. His head cracked against the wall, and he slumped down into an unconscious heap on the ground.

The other wing cracked across the side of Matteaus' head, sending him sprawling to the ground. One of his swords skidded out of reach. Matteaus whipped his head back around and glared at Death. Blood trickled from the corner of his lip, and he spat it at Death's feet. "Come at me."

"I have no time for these games. Kane will hear of this, and you will be no further in the mission you've been facing since the beginning of time. Death waits for no one, Matteaus. Not even you." He bent down and scooped up his robe.

"That's my cue," Tuck whispered. "Do whatever you can to get that feather."

I wrapped my hand around his wrist and pressed my fingers into his skin. "Be careful."

"Always." He winked at me, then forced his fire wings from his back. The whole hallway lit up from his flames.

The angel's head jerked to the side, and his silver eyes went wide. "Phoenix?" He looked between Matteaus and Tuck, then back again. "What is the meaning of this?"

Tuck flapped his wings and flew out into the courtyard at the same time Matteaus jumped to his feet. They ran at the angel from both sides. Tuck's glowing blades grew brighter as he spun them in a circle at his side before clashing with Death. Fire shot from the tips of his swords the second they hit the scythe. Matteaus swung his sword at Death's midsection, drawing his attention away from Tuck.

Death pointed his long, boney finger at Tuck. "It is not yet your time, Phoenix. You must stop this."

My heart was up in my throat, and I was sure I was going to throw up and poop all at the same time. Nervous butterflies fluttered in my stomach. I had to help in some way. I had to do something. I crept to my feet and tiptoed around the outside of the courtyard, making sure to stay under the overhang from the second floor. All the while, Tuck and Matteaus worked together to exchange blows with the angel.

I crawled out to where Grayson lay on the ground. I

crouched over him and shook his shoulder. "Gray. Come on, Gray. Wake up."

His eyelids cracked open. "Did we win?"

"No." His eyes rolled in his head. I tapped the back of my hand against the side of his cheek. "Grayson, I need your speed. Do you understand what I'm saying?"

He held his hand out to me. "Take it."

"You're sure?" I wrapped my fingers with his.

"It's my head that's not right. Just get the blasted feather."

I opened up my magic and felt the first pull off of Grayson. I wasn't supposed to be able to siphon powers from others like him. But here I was letting my powers take over and guide me. The coppery taste of blood filled my mouth, and I felt the overwhelming need to bite something. My vision went from perfect to beyond anything I thought possible. Every particle—every fracture of light—was visible. My sense of smell intensified tenfold. Tucker's warm, woodsy scent hit me, then the sickly-sweet smell of Death, and Matteaus' clean rain smell. Each one was so different, and I was getting them all. I leapt to my feet, and vertigo made my head spin. Was I moving faster than I was before? Only one way to find out.

I crouched down, and the second Death turned his back to me, I ran all out. I ran straight into him, knocking him forward. I quickly backpedaled and found myself five feet away. "Crap."

I pumped my arms and darted forward once more. When I planted my feet, I skidded to a halt, kicking up small pebbles onto the back of Death's legs. He spun in a circle, swinging his scythe out wide.

"Zinnia!" Tuck bellowed.

I threw my arms up and hunched forward. The scythe ran across my wetsuit, and cold air hit my stomach. I pressed my fingers to my skin and looked down. No blood, no cut. *Damn, that was close.* I gave Tuck a thumbs-up, then reached out and grabbed onto Death's wing. Each feather was softer than Matteaus' and felt like silk under my touch. I wrapped my hand around the longest one and pulled with all my might. The feather clung to his wing for a moment, then finally gave way. Death extended his wings out once more, jerking me away from him. I tumbled across the ground and landed flat on my back.

I stuck my hand straight up into the air and waved the feather where Death could not see me. Tuck immediately pulled his swords back and flew to land in a protective stance in front of Niche. I staggered to my feet and hid the feather behind my back as I jogged behind one of the columns. If he didn't feel me pluck it out, I certainly wasn't going to advertise the fact I had it. Matteaus leapt away to stand next to Tuck. He crossed his arms over his chest.

Death stood before them breathless. "Is that all you've got? Come now, Matteaus of the Fallen. I expected much more from a warrior such as yourself."

Matteaus shrugged. "Sorry to disappoint."

"Why? What reason could you have to engage one such as me?" Death's scythe disappeared into thin air as he pulled his cloak back over his shoulder. The ethereal glow of his body was all hidden from view. All but his face.

"I'm here to see that you don't take her." Matteaus nodded down toward Niche's lifeless body.

"I'm afraid that is not for you to decide." Death took a step forward.

"Wait!" Ophelia ran into the courtyard with a vial of a bright purple liquid in her hands. Cross was hot on her heels, holding his sword at the ready. Ophelia didn't even spare him a second look. "It's just a potion. She's not dead."

"I can assure you, my dear. She is dead." Death's face was impassive, as though he was talking about the weather and not the passing of our mentor, the woman who meant so much to us all.

Ophelia dropped down to her knees beside Niche.

"Then you won't mind if I give her this. If she is indeed gone, it shouldn't make a difference."

"You may proceed, Ophelia, daughter of Alataris." Death stood motionless. Not even the wind that blew my hair around could move his.

"How do you know me?" She pulled Niche's head into her lap and pried her mouth open.

"I know many a thing about you. I look forward to seeing which path you choose in the future. Your destiny is the only one among your group that is not yet settled." He tossed his silver hair over his shoulder.

Ophelia uncorked the top of the vial and dumped the contents into Niche's mouth. "What, like everyone else's destiny is set in stone?"

He gave a single nod. "Yes." It was a simple answer, but complicated at the same time. "Many of your brethren here at Evermore Academy have futures no one can see. Not even Death."

Niche's cheeks turned bright pink, and she sat straight up, sucking in a deep breath. She pressed her hands to her chest. "I was really dead."

"Indeed." Death tilted his head to the side, studying her. "How do you feel?"

Her face fell into a mask of anguish, and tears streamed down her face. "It was so . . . just so . . . I can't even describe the peace I felt."

"Rest assured, your time will come, and when it does, I will be here waiting to welcome you with open arms." Death pulled his hood up over his head. "Before I go, I will warn you, Matteaus. I will report to Kane, and things will not be pretty for you."

"Like that's something new." Matteaus waved him away.

Death took a bow. "Until we meet again." Then he disappeared from our sight.

I pulled the feather from behind my back and held it out in front of me. We had an actual real live freaking angel feather. I walked out into the center of the court-yard, holding it like the precious cargo that it was. "We got it."

Niche wrapped her arms around Ophelia's neck and pulled her into a tight hug. "Thank you. I thought I would wake up after taking that."

Ophelia glanced up at me and narrowed her eyes in warning. She pulled back and smiled down at Niche. Ophelia held up the empty vial. "I had an antidote ready just in case."

Niche pulled her into the hug again, and this time Ophelia looked right at me. "You never know what could happen with something like that."

We'd learned the hard way. I nearly died only days ago and drained every one of their powers trying to come back to life. Ophelia helped Niche to her feet, and one by one the rest of the crew came out from their hiding spots. We all met at the center of the courtyard.

I held the feather up. "Looks like we're ready to make one hell of a potion."

Grayson threw his arm over my shoulders and leaned his weight on me. "But who the bloody hell is going to take it? There's not going to be enough for all of us."

Niche shook her head. "Only two can go."

"Then who's it going to be?" Serrina asked the question we were all thinking. "I mean, the potion is supposed to separate the body from the soul so whoever takes it can actually go to the heavenly plane. That's a lot to ask of anyone."

It was the ultimate challenge, one that could go horribly wrong in so many ways. Tuck stood on the other side of the circle with his lips pressed together, and he didn't take his eyes off the ground. In my gut, I felt what he needed to do, what he wanted to do. He was our leader, and he would value that above all else until his duty was complete. When he raised his eyes to meet mine, it was his way of asking me what I wanted him to do here. This wasn't a decision for only one of us. We were in this together. I gave him the smallest nod, so small no one else would see it.

His lips quirked up in that half smile as he lifted his hand ever so slightly. "I'll do it."

"And so will I." The words rushed from my lips, even though I knew this was dangerous, even though we were going to give up our bodies. Where his soul went, so did mine. That was the only thing I was sure of in this crazy life we led.

CHAPTER 28

Deep in the abandoned wing of the Academy, we all walked in two straight lines. Niche gave us the day to shower and rest. Tuck and I had spent the time lying in each other's arms in silence. I stood at the head of one line and Tuck at the other. The weight of the moment pressed down on me, and tension rolled through our crew. No other witch court had gotten this far or dared to attempt what we were about to do. No other supernaturals risked to venture to the heavenly plane—no others but us. I held Hephaestus' sword tight in my hand. It was short, only came to just below my knee, and was surprisingly light. The leather around the hilt was like butter in my hand. So soft and smooth, I felt I could carry it for hours without tiring.

Though the halls were now free of dust, they were

still dark and barely lit. Night had fallen, and with it brought the eerie silence of the abandoned wing. Farther down, the door opened and slammed all at once. Chairs scraped across the ground and hollow laughter filled the air.

Nova sighed. "Well, our resident ghost is in a state tonight."

I didn't turn back to look at her. I just kept on walking. "Why?"

"He seems to think two more spirits will be joining him in being trapped here tonight." Nova cleared her throat. "Not that that's going to happen."

We turned and entered the old classroom we'd been in before. At the center of the pentacle stood a cauldron with a roaring fire under it. The contents bubbled and boiled, sending a rainbow of steam up into the air. Niche waited for us to enter. It was the first time I'd seen her without her lab coat on. Instead, she wore a long white cloak that hung from her shoulders all the way down to the floor. She pointed to each of the five corners of the pentacle. "Queens, each of you take a point. Zinnia, with you at the very top. Knights, stand back."

I took my place at the top of the pentacle. Tuck moved to the back of the room directly across from me. Ophelia held the apple between her hands, Nova held a vial of a swirling silver substance, Serrina held Poseidon's sea glass, and Tabi held the single white feather. I sucked in a deep, calming breath and tightened my grip on the sword. I never thought my soul would leave my body, at least not until I was dead. Now it would, and I would make that trip up to the heavenly plane to do all I could to win this war.

Niche picked up a thick wooden ladle and began stirring the contents of the cauldron. "As you all drop the ingredients into the cauldron, you must repeat the words. *Though the two must separate to find the way through Heaven's gate, I bind the soul to this place. I bind the soul and seal their fate.*"

Ophelia dropped the apple into the cauldron. "Though the two must separate to find the way through Heaven's gate, I bind the soul to this place. I bind the soul and seal their fate." The steam rose from the pot in long golden streams, and the smell of warm apple cider and cinnamon filled the air.

Serrina stepped up and dropped the sea glass into the cauldron. "Though the two must separate to find the way through Heaven's gate, I bind the soul to this place. I bind the soul and seal their fate." The glass dipped down into the hot liquid for only a moment before it melted together and rose up out of the golden steam. The molten glass rotated around the steam like one of

267

Saturn's rings. It was a beautiful sheer blue that twisted and turned in all different directions.

Tabi stepped up next. "Though the two must separate to find the way through Heaven's gate, I bind the soul to this place. I bind the soul and seal their fate." She tossed the feather into the boiling substance, and the sound of tinkering bells filled the room. White puffs of smoke drifted like clouds to mix with the other ingredients.

Lastly, Nova held her vial over the pot. She uncorked the top, and I swear I heard screaming. She turned it over to pour it into the cauldron, but the contents couldn't come out. She banged on the back of the bottle. Still nothing. Finally, she snapped her fingers, and purple sparks flew from the tips of her fingers into the bottle, drawing out the shimmering ghostly white liquid. It seeped from the bottle like maple syrup and fell into the cauldron. "Though the two must separate to find the way through Heaven's gate, I bind the soul to this place. I bind the soul and seal their fate."

The contents exploded out of the pot and straight into the air. The sea glass spun around like a twister coming together to form a V-shaped bowl. Above the container, the liquid dripped down into it one drop at a time. I held my breath, watching, waiting for it to be complete. The bowl filled to the top with contents that bubbled with multicolored glitter.

Niche dropped the ladle into the empty pot and lifted her arms up, plucking the bowl from where it floated. "Now, my queens, each of you must filter some of your power to Zinnia. She's going to need all she can get."

They held their hands out toward me. One by one they let their magic go. I opened my arms and my powers to them, letting it seep into me—Tabi's ribbons of yellow, Serrina's red streams, Nova's purple sparks, and Ophelia's dark smoke. They mixed with mine, and my body flooded with power. It coursed through my veins, ready to be used at any time. It filled every part of me. An array of color mixed with my glittering silver powers. It streamed down my arms and all through my hair.

Niche motioned for Tuck to step up and join us. "This way."

The others stepped back, looking more drained than ever, but they were wide awake—more awake than any other time they'd given me their power.

Niche held the bowl out to me. "Are you sure about this?"

I looked Tuck dead in the eye. "I'm sure." I took the bowl from her hands and held it up to my lips. I tipped it back before I could change my mind and sipped the thick liquid. It tasted of the sweetest milkshake and the sourest apple, the spiciest pepper and the smoothest pudding. My body felt like it was fire and ice all at once. I staggered back.

"Zinnia?" Tucker grabbed the bowl from my hand and chugged the rest of the liquid down. He reached out and wrapped his arm around my back and pulled me closer. "Are you okay?"

I'd never felt anything like that before. I was drunk on power, so much power it practically burst from my skin. I waited to lose consciousness, expected to find myself standing over my lifeless body. Instead, my skin glowed even brighter, like I had a spotlight shining from within. Tuck lit up like a Christmas tree. We both looked down at ourselves.

I felt everything around me, the pulse of the earth, every heartbeat coming from my friends. I heard students' movements coming from the other side of the school.

Niche moved next to us. She pressed her hand to my forehead, then looked deep into my eyes. "This isn't right. Something's not right here." She turned to Nova. "Where did you get that essence of soul?"

Nova shrugged. "I may or may not have taken it from the pits of Tartarus."

"You stole the essence from the soul of a Titan?" She narrowed her eyes at Nova. "Great. Just great. The one time I am not specific . . . the one time . . . and now look what happened!"

I was calmer than ever.

Tuck placed his hand on Niche's arm. "Everything is going to be okay."

"Oh, no, it's not." Niche shook her head. "You were supposed to be separated from your bodies. You were supposed to be spirits."

I felt better than ever, and I still had my body. "Does this mean we can't go to the heavenly plane?"

"Oh, you can go anywhere you want right now." She pursed her lips and rolled her eyes at Nova.

Tuck rocked back on his heels and up to his toes. "So, what's the problem?"

"Ugh, the problem is she made you into freaking Greeks. You're just as powerful as they are now . . . maybe more."

Tuck and I looked at each other, drunk with power, so much power I could barely contain myself. His lips pulled into that familiar cocky grin. "Well, what do you want to do now?"

I held my hand up and let a ball of all-powerful magic form just above my palm. It twisted and swirled with light of all different colors. With the other, I lifted the sword and light glinted off the blade. I smiled. *Game changer!* "Now? I say, let's go get us a crown."

I HOPE you enjoyed reading the first steps leading up to the epic battle between Alataris and our Queen Witches. To find out what happens to Zinnia's mother and if Tuck and Zinnia finally reveal their love to the world keep on reading. The fifth book in The Royals: Witch Court, *Wicked Queen*, is releasing summer 2019 and is available for order now just CLICK HERE!

Turn the page to the cover for *Wicked Queen*!

To order *Wicked Queen* CLICK HERE!

My power, my reign...

I thought I knew danger, I was wrong. That wicked potion was just the beginning. I feel strong with Tuck by my side, but we're in way over our heads. We need heavenly Fire. It's the only thing that can destroy Alataris' crown. And we can't beat him any other way. That crown is the seat of his power...and I'm going to take it from him.

This is my deadliest mission yet, but I'm out of options and out of time. I have to stop running from him and face my father head on with everything I've got. He thinks he'll win, he thinks I'll buckle after he summons the ultimate evil. But he has no idea what I'd do to protect the people I love. I will take him down, even if I die with him.

This is a family affair and it's time I show my father just how Wicked a Queen can be...

To clam a throne I'll have to embrace the dark side of my powers...Nothing will ever be the same.

To order *Wicked Queen* CLICK HERE!

GET ready for your next dose of *magic* in season two of *The Royals: Warlock Court Book 1*! To order Wicked Omen Click Here!

There's no such thing as magical powers.

Most orphans grow up in foster homes not penthouse suites on the Upper East Side. Everyone always tells me how lucky I am. I know they're right, and I am grateful...but I don't belong here. It all feels so...empty.

In the pit of my stomach I know there has to be more to the world than this. The money, the spoiled rich life doesn't feel like my own. Darkness lingers all around me and I feel it's draw. It sings to me like a siren's song and I've lost the willpower to ignore it.

And then he shows up. His name is Beckett Dust, and he's infuriating. Drop dead gorgeous, but he makes my blood boil. He tells me of a secret world hiding in plain sight, one of magic and power. He paints a pretty picture of a life I'd always dreamed of then takes me to a magical academy to train for a war I have to fight. I'm surrounded by people who want me to fail and he is nowhere to be found.

I'm in over my head and now... they want to use me as

a weapon.

To order Wicked Omen Click Here!

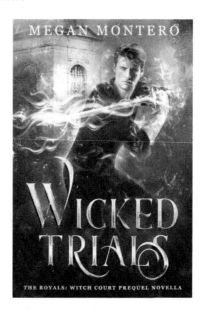

THIS POWER CHOSE *ME*...

Within the supernatural world of Evermore everyone prays their child will be born with the Mark of the Guardian for they have unparalleled strength, intelligence, and *power*...but they have no idea what it's actually like. I didn't wish for this *gift* and I definitely don't want it. I was born a prince, I already had it all. This Mark on my neck stole all of it from me and forced me into a dangerous life I'd gladly trade away if I could...

But now the Witch Queens have ascended and it's time to try and defeat the evil King once and for all. For over a thousand years his cruelty has spared no one as his torturous power grows stronger. He must be stopped now, before his reign destroys everything and anything in his way. So I must push aside my dreams of returning home to the family that cast me out. I must step up and claim the power that chose me. I *must* enter the Trials and become a Knight in the Witch's Court.

There's only one way to prevent the tyrannical king from destroying everything I love…I must become the one thing he can't beat.

The magic continues with *Wicked Omen*! The first book in season two *The Royals: Warlock Court*. To pre-order *Wicked Omen* CLICK HERE.

The magic continues in *Wicked Magic*! CLICK HERE to order *Wicked Magic*.

WANT to see Zinnia's first days in the wicked world of Evermore. Click here to get your copy of *Wicked Witch.*

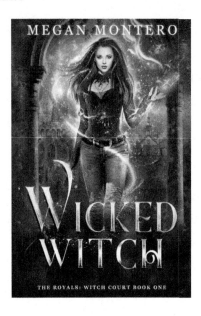

It's time to claim my power...

All my life I've lived under lock and key, always following the strict rules my mother set for me. A week before my sixteenth birthday I sneak out of my house and discover *why*. Turns out I am not just a normal teenager. I'm a witch blessed with a gift someone wants to steal from me.

And not just anyone...*the* evil King Alataris.

For a thousand years the people of Evermore have suffered under his tyranny. The Mark on my shoulder says I am the Siphon Witch, one of five Witch Queens fated to come together and finally destroy him. The only thing keeping Evermore safe is the Stone that shields the witch kingdoms from Alataris's magic…and now he's found a way to steal it. Suddenly, I'm sent on a quest to find the ancient spell to protect the Stone. My only hope for surviving is through my strikingly beautiful and immensely powerful Guardian, Tucker. The laws of Evermore state that love between us is strictly forbidden, and it appears I'm the only one willing to give in to the attraction…

When the quest turns more dangerous than expected I realize I have absolutely no idea what I'm doing. I was raised *human*. But I have to learn my magic fast because If King Alataris gets his hands on me he'll steal my magic *and* my life…but if he gets his hands on the stone we *all* die.

THEY ALL FEAR MY POWER...THEY should.

FINDING out I'm a witch was a shock. But now that I'm in the world of Evermore I'll do anything to protect it even if that means dying...

The evil King Alataris has stolen my mother, my life, and now he's taken something that could unleash hell on earth. With a powerful Ice Dragon under his every command there is no telling where he will strike next. The Witch Queens have been tasked with saving Evermore. The only problem? The others fear the wild, powerful nature of my magic and sometimes so do I!

The only one who can help me contain it is my protective Knight, Tucker Brand. But even he has his own set of secrets. My feelings for him are overwhelming and strictly forbidden, if we give into the fire we share for even a moment we will lose everything.

When it comes time to take back what Alataris has stolen we set out on our most perilous mission yet. To save the Dragon and Evermore before it's too late. If we fail, the world as we know it will come to an end…and all will be lost for Evermore.

CLICK HERE To order Wicked Magic!

CHECK out Zinnia and Tuck's biggest struggle yet in *Wicked Hex*. CLICK HERE to order *Wicked Hex*.

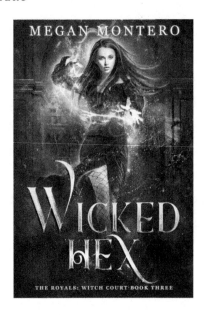

SOME POWERS COME WITH A PRICE...

My life is unrecognizable. I've never been in more danger. I thought I was safe at Evermore Academy. I thought we were finally making progress in this war. I thought I was safe within these walls.

I thought I could always count on Tucker...I thought wrong.

But Now all that's changed. Alataris is coming for me with everything he's got, and no one is safe. He's using the ones I love against me. I'm not sure who is on my side or who has fallen to the enemy's tricks. I want to turn to Tuck, but even he is hiding things from me.

My life is falling to pieces and to fix it I'll have to turn to the one person I know I can't trust...

Click Here to Order *Wicked Hex!*

FOR THE LATEST NEWS, events and to get free books join my newsletter simply Click Here!

WANT to connect with me and other fans of Evermore? Click Here to join my reader group on Facebook!

DID you read the prequel novella *Wicked Trials?* Do you want to learn how Tucker and his knights got started? Great News- it's FREE- if you sign up for my news-letter! Click Here to sign up and start getting WICKED with your free ebook now!

ABOUT THE AUTHOR

Megan Montero was born and raised as sassy Jersey girl. After devouring series like the Immortals After Dark, the Arcana Chronicles, Harry Potter and Mortal Instruments she decided then and there at she would write her own series. When she's not putting pen to paper you can find her cuddled up under a thick blanket (even in the summer) with a book in her hands. When she's not reading or writing you can find her playing with her dogs, watching movies, listening to music or moving the furniture around her house…again. She loves finding magic in all aspects of her life and that's why she writes Urban Fantasy and Paranormal.

Learn about Megan and her books by visiting her website at:

Www.meganmontero.com

Printed in Great Britain
by Amazon